The Big Sugar

Also by Mary Logue
Published by the University of Minnesota Press

The Streel: A Deadwood Mystery

The
BIG SUGAR

A
Brigid Reardon
Mystery

MARY LOGUE

University of Minnesota Press
Minneapolis ✻ London

The epigraphs for the book are from *Cowboy Songs and Other Frontier Ballads,* compiled by John A. Lomax and originally published in 1910.

Published by the University of Minnesota Press
111 Third Avenue South, Suite 290
Minneapolis, MN 55401–2520
http://www.upress.umn.edu

ISBN 978-1-5179-1369-4 (hc)
ISBN 978-1-5179-1370-0 (pb)

Library of Congress record available at https://lccn.loc.gov/2022052947

Printed in the United States of America on acid-free paper

The University of Minnesota is an equal-opportunity educator and employer.

30 29 28 27 26 25 24 23   10 9 8 7 6 5 4 3 2 1

Contents

Prologue

I'll sing you a song, though it may be a sad one,
Of trials and troubles and where they first begun;
I left my dear kindred, my friends, and my home,
Across the wild deserts and mountains to roam.

—*Cowboy Songs*

Cheyenne, Wyoming Territory
May 1881

Sitting high in the saddle, I could see for miles over the flat and unfamiliar land. Not a tree in sight. The range, as the cowboys called it, was wide open with a fierce wind kicking up dust devils. Neither human nor animal moved in this stark and empty landscape. What seemed most alive were the clouds as they swirled and streaked across the sky.

This great openness gave me both a sense of immense freedom and the touch of fear that often comes along with no boundaries. All I could see in the far distance were the Rocky Mountains, looking much like a giant hand pressing down on the earth. I had never before seen mountains of such magnitude. The Black Hills were just that in comparison—hills.

In the country of my birth, my Ireland, the mountains came close and the clouds hovered so that one felt swaddled and protected. And the color of them was the deepest green, for they were covered with life. But the

Rockies were formed from molten dark stone pushed out of the Earth and seemed deep purple and impenetrable from a distance.

In the Wyoming Territory there often appeared to be little green; the plains spread out like they were never ending and one could get lost in them so easily. In an odd way, the land reminded me of the sea, stretching out with no end in sight. And the mountains rose up like *mada doininne,* dark clouds that formed on the horizon. In English they would be called "hounds of the storm."

The few plants I could see were odd thorny creatures, of a dull sage color—"cactus," they were called. When the occasional tree appeared, it looked skeletal and lonely. I shivered as I looked over this land that was my new home.

*   *   *

Earlier, when I was getting ready for my first foray out to the plains, Padraic had asked me to wait until he could ride with me, but, this once, I wanted to be on my own.

My brother Seamus and I had met Padraic and his partner Billy on the boat coming over from Galway. That was three years ago, when I was but sixteen. The three of them went off on the rails and ended up mining in the Black Hills, while I stayed behind in New York, then got a job as a house maid in St. Paul, Minnesota. From there I managed to make my way and join them all in Deadwood, in the southern part of the Dakota Territory. That lasted but a few days, as a young woman was killed and my brother blamed for her death.

When my brother escaped to Cheyenne and Billy died, Padraic decided it was up to him to watch over me. Not that I asked him to. He couldn't get over trying to protect me, and I didn't always care for the way he hovered about me.

We had been together too much. Even if he had been, as we claimed, my brother, I would have grown tired of his overbearing concern for me. Which did not mean I did not love him.

So it was, on my first ride outside the paddock with Grian, my three-year-old filly, that I saw in the distance a small stand of trees.

✳   ✳   ✳

At first the green oasis was a welcome sight on the dusty land. I so missed trees. The faint lime color of the cottonwood's new leaves was a refreshing sight and gave promise to the coming spring. I wondered if there might be a pool of water there, a spring that had allowed this greenness to grow. I touched Grian into a trot and headed toward the oasis, hoping to water my horse and take a brief rest.

As I approached, a flash of white caught my eye. At first I was sure it was some high-flying bird—a hawk, maybe even an eagle—come to land in the tree, but its movements were quite odd.

On second glance, I could see that caught among the branches near the bottom of the cottonwood tree was a petticoat flying up in the wind. How had it come to be there?

My heart leapt into my throat. A petticoat. Whatever for? The whiteness of it seemed so out of place.

When I rode closer, I cried out at what I was seeing: the petticoat was floating around a body and the body was twirling at the end of a rope.

I reined in my horse and took in the sight.

A woman (could she be called that still?) was swaying in the wind as her body hung from the tree branches. I felt chilled to the bone by such a horrible and impossible sight imprinted on my every nerve. *No, no, no!* I shouted in my head. *No, please make this go away!*

Everything in me screamed to turn Grian around and ride as hard and fast as I could back to safety—away from what I did not want to see—but instead I forced my horse forward.

Grian must have sensed my dismay as she shied.

I tightened the reins to calm her; she danced but then settled. Patting her, I leaned over her neck and whispered in Gaelic to tell her what a good girl she was, "*Nighean mhath.*"

I advanced a few paces nearer so I could see who was dangling from the rope, her head bobbing forward like a rag doll's. A slight cast of darkness seemed to have fallen over her features, but I could see that it was my neighbor Ella. I was horrified. Her mouth hung open and her eyes were staring straight ahead, to a future she would never see. Her arms were pulled behind her, and her dress was lifting in the wind as if it were all that was still alive. Her feet were not even a foot or so above the ground, which emphasized the cruelty of this act. Life was only that close, but not close enough.

For a moment I wondered if she could have done this to herself. When I last saw her, Ella had seemed happy enough—surely, it was I who was crying when we first met. Wouldn't she have mentioned her own troubles if they were this unbearable?

But then I knew what had happened to her, for her hands were tied behind her back. And I knew what I was seeing. It was clear she could not have done this to herself, so it was not a suicide.

I forced myself to look at her face.

She had been murdered.

❋   ❋   ❋

Ever since Padraic and I had arrived in Cheyenne from Deadwood, I had heard such awful killings happened here but had hoped never to see one. The lawlessness of this vast country was beyond comprehension. When I left Deadwood, I was hoping to leave some of such violence behind me, but here I was staring at a murder again.

What could she have done that would have caused this to happen? What person had she crossed that needed to be avenged? I couldn't imagine.

I had to leave her as I found her, but it was an awful feeling to not be able to take care of her body. But I thought it would be wise to bring the sheriff out to see for himself how her death had been forced on her.

Just at the edge of the trees, I pulled Grian to a stop, wrapped the reins around the pommel of the saddle, and slid off her back. I couldn't look back, but I had to take a moment to gather myself before going forward.

I didn't want this to be, and me the one to find her. I didn't want to see what I was seeing. Leaning my head into the velvet of Grian's neck, I sought comfort, for I had hoped to have the poor woman now hanging in the tree as a friend. The tears I shed were not just for the death of this woman, but for me too. How does one go forward having witnessed such a horrible scene? How was I to continue in this place?

Like us, she was a newcomer to the territory. She had staked a homestead a year or two earlier and was running a small herd of cattle. I had eaten her hardtack and talked with her. Our closest neighbor, she had already built a wooden shack for a home with her partner. I had even visited her home.

And now she had been strung up and left for the vultures.

Part I

Cheyenne

Where the air is so pure, the zephyrs so free,
The breezes so balmy and light,
That I would not exchange my home on the range
For all of the cities so bright.

* * *

Oh, I love these wild flowers in this dear land of ours,
The curlew I love to hear scream,
And I love the white rocks and the antelope flocks
That graze on the mountain-tops green.

—*Cowboy Songs*

1

April 1881

When I stepped down from the Black Hills stagecoach onto the firm ground of our destination, Cheyenne, I thought my legs would give out from under me. During the past few days I had used them so infrequently. Padraic and I had finally arrived late in the afternoon of our fourth day of travel from Deadwood, with only a one-night stop to get out of the coach and rest in a bed. The horses were luckier than we were: they were changed every day.

As we had traveled across the plains, there were still remnants of old snow in the hollows, but the wind was blowing warm, a Chinook, the driver called it. He assured us that the snow wouldn't last long.

How glad I was to get sight of this new place, a booming town in the Wyoming Territory. After Deadwood, a small town tucked into the mountains, it felt good to be on wide streets with the sky above a huge blue canopy. I was working on being hopeful, praying that we would find our way in this frontier place, but once again, I felt totally out of my depths.

Most important to me was to be reunited with my dear brother Seamus. He left Deadwood when he was accused of the murder of a saloon girl, his own fiancée. All we knew was that Cheyenne had been his destination. I couldn't wait to find him and hoped that he had stayed put once he had reached this fair city. I couldn't wait to tell him all the good news—that he was no longer wanted for that savage act, which had been blamed on another, and that we had sold the mine and made a small fortune. The money had been wired to the Western Union office in Cheyenne and was waiting for us to sign for it. It was more money than we had ever known.

Cheyenne might be a good place to spend some of that money if I ended up staying here for a time. The town was said to be up-and-coming, as the Union Pacific railroad had recently arrived there from out East. This made Cheyenne an end-of-the-tracks town with a population close to five thousand people. Or so I had been told. Also, women who were older than twenty-one years and citizens of the territory now had the right to vote in the Wyoming Territory. When I reached that grand old age, I'd be happy to stand in line for this privilege. I wondered when the next election would be and what it would all involve.

As I looked down the muddy thoroughfare I saw building after building, most of them brick and at least two-story, with mansard roofs. Wagonloads of goods were being driven down the streets pulled by two to four horses, and people were crowding the sidewalks. A boomtown, indeed.

Padraic busied himself getting our luggage down from the upper racks of the stagecoach. We had not traveled light, taking with us all that we might need to set up life in a new town. I could hear the pots and pans clanging in the basket he put at my feet.

Farther down the street, my eyes lit on an enormous brick building, the size of which I hadn't seen since I had worked in St. Paul, Minnesota. A veranda circled the front and the sides, half a story up from the wooden sidewalk. Rocking chairs lined the railing, and I saw a few men sitting in them, smoking cigars, with their broad-brimmed hats pushed back on their foreheads.

Were they cowboys? I wondered. I was looking forward to seeing these wild men of the West.

Cheyenne was called the "magic city of the plains" and viewing that elegant building I did not doubt the name. If only we would find some of that magic—and also my brother Seamus. It was rumored he had joined up with a bunch of cowhands who were stabled at a ranch just outside Cheyenne. It was all I could do to not immediately start asking around for him.

Instead, I turned and asked the stagecoach driver what that big grand building might be.

"Oh, yeah, that's quite the place, I hear. Never been in it myself. It's the Cheyenne Club, very swanky and exclusive to the big sugars around here, only two hundred are allowed to be members. It's a pretty fancy place for this rough-and-tumble town. But then, Cheyenne is the capital of this here territory."

"May anyone go into the club?" I asked, curious to see its interior and wishing to see some civilization. Maybe I could go in and ask about Seamus; it seemed like the kind of place where people would be in the know.

"From what I've heard you can go in only if you've got an invite from one of the big sugars."

That was a term I had never heard before, but it rolled off his tongue like I should know it. "And who are these *big sugars*?"

"That's what they call the cattle barons around these parts. They're the fellas with the money, and I guess that makes them sweet."

I wondered what chance I'd have to meet one of these big sugars and wrangle an invitation to that fancy club. Padraic came up behind me and slid an arm around my shoulders. "We're here. We made it."

I looked up at him, trying not to sound too anxious. "So I see. But how are we going to find Seamus in this big place? He could be anywhere."

"Well, I won't start looking there. I doubt he'd be found in that fancy place." Padraic waved an arm at the Cheyenne Club. "And I don't think we'll be enjoying the lodging of such a grand estate."

"No, but we do need to find some lodging for at least a few nights." I felt a slight shiver of apprehension, praying that our travels weren't in vain. "And after that maybe Seamus will have some place we can stay."

With every trip I took, I moved farther and farther away from Ireland. My brother felt like the last link to my family, and I couldn't bear the thought of not being able to find him. I repeated myself: "We'll need to find a place to stay until we find Seamus and know what's what."

"You stay here with the bags and I'll ask around town for a nice, clean place for a decent lady like you. Don't worry. I'll take good care of you— even after we find that no-good brother of yours."

Watching him walk away, I felt confused about what he meant to me. He was so familiar, in many ways like a brother. I couldn't figure out if I loved him or just needed him to be close. I knew he was good to the core, and really, what more could a woman want in a husband? I just wasn't sure of my own feelings. Nor was I clear that he was sure of his.

I sat down on one of the trunks and watched the people walk by. Even I could pick out by their dress who were the cowboys and who were the cattle barons. The well-dressed men doffed their hats, but the cowboys just nodded, as if their sombrero-like hats were meant to never leave their heads. The cowboys looked tough, wearing leather chaps, with red bandannas tied around their necks. Their tall boots with spurs jingled as they strode bowlegged down the streets. They walked as if they owned the place.

How might I appear to them, sitting alone on the sidewalk in my second-best dress and a rough woolen shawl I had knit myself? My hair was relatively tidy, pushed back under my hat, and my boots were only slightly muddy. But I hadn't looked at myself in more than four days, no mirrors being handy. A blessing, possibly.

"May I be of assistance?" a man asked behind me. "Are you waiting for someone?"

I turned and saw I was being addressed by a tall man in a fine suitcoat wearing a handsome felt hat, one much cleaner than the cowboys'. He had a neatly trimmed silver beard and was even sporting a tie. He gave me a slight bow, which came off as if he were mocking me and my position perched on a trunk in the middle of the wooden sidewalk.

Words almost tumbled out of my mouth that indeed I was looking for my brother, but I held them back. There was something about the man that made me think twice, an air as if he could give me anything I wished for but there would be a cost. And for that matter, I did not like the way he was looking at me at all.

"Thank you, but I'm fine. My brother has gone off to find us rooms." I looked down, hoping he would not see through my lie. I felt uneasy talking to a strange man and wanted him to move on.

Instead he came closer and stared me up and down. "So you're new to our booming town?"

"Yes, as you can see." I pointed out our luggage. "We've just arrived."

"Welcome to our fine city. What brings you to Cheyenne?" he asked, this time removing his hat.

I wasn't sure I wanted this sly gentleman to know too much about me. So I just said, "We might be just passing through. We'll have to see."

"I hear by your accent that you are Irish. There are many such people here, and the ones who are hard workers have made a go of it. You can, too."

I wasn't sure if that was a compliment, but I thanked him anyway.

"Well, I noticed you were looking at our new establishment, the

Cheyenne Club. Our association just finished the building of it this past year. All of us ranchers went in together to make it a place where we can relax and enjoy what we've earned. We just celebrated its opening this year. I declare the club is the finest in existence. None can outdo it, be it in Chicago or New York."

"It is indeed a fine building," I assured him.

He smiled at my words as if he alone were responsible for its grandeur. "I'm glad you think so. Perhaps someday I might have the pleasure of showing you around the premises, Miss."

Surprised by his familiarity—and by his assumption that I was unmarried—I again didn't know how to respond so I simply murmured, "Perhaps."

"Pardon me for not introducing myself. I am Albert Bothwell, and I have a nice little spread just outside of town." He doffed his hat.

I wasn't sure what a spread was, but I guessed it was a farm of some sort. "My name is Brigid Reardon, and as I said, I'm waiting for my brother to return. We've had a long journey."

"Where have you come from?"

"Deadwood."

"Oh, so many are heading up there hoping to find their fortune."

I allowed myself a small smile. "We've already sold our mine." I couldn't help bragging a bit. But I wanted to talk of Deadwood no more, for we had left under a bit of a cloud.

At my words, his eyes lit up. "Good for you. With your family?"

"Yes, with my brothers," I told him.

"And you are a miss, I hope?"

"At the moment," I snapped, disliking his impertinence.

He laughed. "Pleased to make your acquaintance, Miss Reardon. Do you perhaps have a *carte de visite*?"

I knew what that was, but I also knew those were used by the swells and courtesans, not by a young Irish girl like me. I wasn't sure I wanted this inquisitive man to be visiting me anyway.

"Not at present," I responded.

I looked up to see Padraic loping down the street. He was, as always, a most welcome sight.

"And here comes my brother now. Thanks for your concern," I said, not wanting to be outdone in politeness but desiring the man to leave me be.

"I'm sure we will meet again," Bothwell said with a smooth smile. Taking his leave, he strode away.

I turned to get the news from Padraic, hoping that he wouldn't have noticed that a strange man had been talking to me. He was already so protective, and I wanted to give him no good reason to be more so. But sure enough, when he came up to me the first words out of his mouth were "Who was that man you were talking to?"

"Oh, Padraic, how did it go? Were you able to find a room?" I asked, trying to divert him.

"Yes, in a fine place, but who was that man? I can't leave you alone without you attracting attention. Was he bothering you?"

"No, not at all. He was just trying to be of assistance. He was telling me a bit about the town."

Padraic lifted one of our bags, then said in a cynical tone, "I'm sure that's all he wanted."

I would not argue with Padraic, for I was not sure what the man's intentions had been, nor did I want to find out.

2

Without much trouble, Padraic hailed a man passing by with a cart to take our luggage to the hotel. The two men loaded our four trunks on the cart and then Padraic led the way.

As we walked along, he told me, "I asked around and everyone said we should stay at Dyer's Hotel. The owner is Irish so I guessed that might suit us just fine. We get breakfast and dinner, and there's a full bath down the hall, with running water. And it's a very clean establishment. I think you'll approve."

"A real bath, imagine. I'm taking a long soak tonight." Then I asked, knowing full well that he wouldn't have checked, "Did you see the rooms?"

"No, but I'm sure it's fine."

I caught his hesitation at my question and had to ask, "Padraic, did you just get one room?"

"Do we have need of more?" he asked, walking faster now. "I think we must watch our money until we are able to get our payment from the Hunts."

"Yes, I agree, tomorrow we must deal with the money Mr. Hunt has sent us. I will not feel comfortable until we have it in hand and then put most of it safely locked away in a bank. We'll be as rich as we'll ever be."

"I wouldn't be so sure of that," Padraic laughed. "Who knows? We might get richer."

"But is it proper for us to share a room?" I asked, knowing it wasn't proper but wondering what he thought about it.

"I've said that you are my sister. Surely that will make it fine. You'll be safe with me."

"Safe? Your sister? Tell me true, Padraic, is that how you think of me?" I teased him.

"You know I don't think of you that a way." He squeezed my arm. "Will it be okay? It won't be for long, I don't think."

"As long as there are two beds," I assured him.

"I'm sure there will be."

I shook my head. "Oh, Padraic, I swear. I'm sure of nothing. I should have gone myself."

We had been having a teasing argument about what our living arrangement would be when we arrived in Cheyenne. He even suggested we say we were married, just to make things easier. In answer to his suggestion, I told him clearly that I was not ready to even think of that. Instead he would be my brother.

Even if I did want to marry him—and the thought had occurred to me—I just wasn't sure. Besides, I would need my real brother to be present, my only family I had in this far country. I thought of my poor mother gone to the grave and me with no father here to give me away. But Seamus would do. And I would want to be married in a Catholic church by an ordained priest. Just because we were living out in a wilderness was no reason to be uncivilized about the way such things should be done.

When I told him this, Padraic had laughed like he was just joking, which was no response at all. I didn't really know what he wanted with me. I could tell he cared about me, but he could also be rather distant and standoffish. Padraic had his moods, I guess you could say. Being his sister for the time being might not be such a bad thing while I made up my mind about him.

And come to think of it, he about me.

❉   ❉   ❉

When we arrived at Dyer's Hotel, I was taken aback by the glamour of it all. I hadn't expected this from the way Padraic had spoken about it. Sure and maybe it wasn't as fine as the Intercontinental Hotel, the fanciest place in town that we had heard so much about on our travels, but it was the first time that I would stay in a place where you dressed and came down to dinner.

I stared at the ceiling, which seemed very high and had a painting of the sky on it, which made it seem even higher. The lobby rose two floors, with marble pillars, and a dark wood balustrade led to the second floor. The marble floors had large oriental rugs laid across them, so beautiful I hated to walk on them.

A man ran to us to help with our trunks. He wore a uniform, and Padraic told me he was called a bellboy, but the man certainly wasn't young enough to be a boy. We were staying on the second floor, and it took two of the bellmen to carry our trunks up the stairs.

The room was simple enough. To my relief it had two single beds, one by the window and the other close to the door.

"How much did this cost, then?" I asked.

"A dollar a day, but that includes two meals. We surely can afford it. We'll get our money tomorrow. Let's enjoy this luxury tonight."

I walked to the bed by the window and stretched out on the finely woven coverlet, claiming it for myself. It felt immeasurably good to be prone after such a long time jouncing around in the stagecoach.

"The first thing we'll do is to ask about Seamus," I stated.

"Yes, we'll get the lay of the land, find that no-good brother of yours, and settle into a place we can call home, at least for a while." Padraic tried to sound assured of all he was saying, but there was a quaver in his voice.

I turned toward him. "Paddy?"

He was perched on the edge of the other bed, his hat in his hands, worrying the rim of it.

"Don't worry," I told him.

"I just hope that money is waiting for us. What if that Mr. Hunt decided to pull a fast one on us?"

"I don't think he would do that, given what we know of his son. I think they are deceiving people, but not thieves."

"You knew them best."

"We'll be fine," I said.

He looked over at me, heaved a sigh, then smiled and said, "With you around, dear sister of mine, we'll be more than fine."

I reached back and threw my pillow at him.

3

To bathe in a real, full-sized bathtub felt like such a luxury after scrubbing down in a tin bucket in our Deadwood kitchen. I sank into the water, letting it cradle my tired and dirty body. I was alone in a small bathroom down the hall from our room. I hadn't had running water since I worked for the Hunt family in St. Paul. And even there, the tub in the servants' quarters was nowhere as near as nice as this. This tub was as white as white could be and smooth to the touch. I luxuriated in it.

Padraic had chosen well. In this hotel even the soap was fancy with a fragrance of roses. I could have soaked in the porcelain tub the rest of the night, but I was that hungry too.

When I walked back to the room, having pulled my coat around me for decency, Padraic smiled at me and then quickly left the room so I could change into a dress. I stared at the four dresses in my trunk, all I had to choose from: a nice, plain two-piece that Mrs. Hill had given me, a flannel one I bought secondhand in Deadwood, a gingham one I had remade myself from an older one I had worn on the journey from Ireland. Finally, there was my ball gown that I had worn only once, on a night I would never forget or want to remember. All I had wanted to do was dance that night away in Deadwood. And when I danced that night with Padraic, I began to see him not as a friend of my brother, not as merely a partner in the mine, but as a possibility. The way he had held me told more than any words could have.

But that night I also danced with Charlie Hunt, the rich man who was going to buy our mine, and who I had had my eye on. It had all been so confusing but became even more so when I was abducted from the dance and woke to find myself in a railroad tunnel underground. I shivered in the cool air, remembering how I had managed to escape from the tunnel and make my way to the priest's house. Why was I thinking of all this? I had to get ready for dinner.

I chose the flannel gown, as it had gone rather chilly, and I dressed it up with the paisley shawl that had been a gift too. My hair I pulled back, but I let a few tendrils frame my face. I hoped I was well enough attired to be served in the fancy dining room.

Padraic had taken his clothes into the bathroom with him and re-entered our room wearing his one remaining clean shirt and his wrinkled wool trousers. He slipped on his old worn-out vest to complete his ensemble.

"No other pants?" I asked.

"These will do."

Seeing that even his clean shirt was fraying on the cuffs, I said, "In that case, I will put new clothes on our shopping list for tomorrow. When we finally have money to spend."

"My, Brigid, but you look grand."

"Put some decent clothes on you and you wouldn't be bad-looking yourself." I noticed he had taken the time to trim up his beard. I liked it better that way—short and styled.

"I could eat a bear," he said.

"They might well serve it here."

❉   ❉   ❉

But we did not see bear listed when we were handed menus.

I was surprised that we were being waited on by a young woman; usually men were the waiters. Recently I had heard that as the railroads came west a man named Fred Harvey was hiring girls to work at his restaurants. One more attraction for all the men who built the railroads was surely the Harvey Girls.

Our waitress was a lovely young woman who had also come over from Ireland. We found out she had lived not far from Galway, close to where I had lived. Like the men waiters, she was dressed in black. She wore a simple dress with a starched white apron over it. Her name, she told us, was

Molly—actually, she really told that only to Padraic. I could tell she had taken a shine to him. At first he didn't seem to notice, as he was studying the menu, which I hoped he was able to read. I had started to teach him to read and write when we were in Deadwood. He was coming along nicely.

But then Padraic looked up and smiled at her. He told her his name, then turned to me and added, "And this is my sister, Brigid."

I wanted to kick him under the table for that. There was no need for him to give this saucy young woman any more information about the two of us than was necessary for her to know. Padraic didn't notice my discontent. He turned back to the menu and studied it hard. He had reached the point where he didn't like me to help him anymore, so I let him examine the menu as long as he needed.

"Sir," Molly said politely. "Would you like something to drink?"

"Yes, any beer would be grand."

"We serve Jacques Braun's. It's from the brewery just down the street. I'm sure you'll find it to your liking."

At this Padriac looked up again and gave her another full-hearted smile. "Well, if you say so, then."

She blushed and turned to me. "And for you, ma'am?"

I started at being called a ma'am—we were surely the same age. But maybe that's what the servers were taught here. "I'll have a glass of wine." I felt that in an elegant hotel like this one should drink something better than beer.

"We just have the red, and I know nothing about it."

"That will be fine."

Looking over the menu I decided to be adventurous and ordered the antelope. Remembering them running across the plains, I wondered if the meat would be tough with so much muscle on the beast. Padraic ordered the chicken, saying he didn't need to try anything new, thank you very much.

Our food came out fast and was laid on the plate in a most elegant way. We each had sides of potatoes and cabbage, which I knew would make Padraic feel right at home. The meat on my plate looked like a cut of beef, and I found it surprisingly tender. Padraic ate his chicken so fast it liked to slide down his throat with no chewing. He was as hungry as I was, but I did try to temper my eating.

As we were finishing our fare, a small dark-haired man, dressed in a full suit with a dark-red paisley cravat, came to our table and clapped his hands together, startling both of us. He laughed. "I hear you're from the old country," he said in a brogue as thick as they come.

"Not so old," I said back, to tease him a bit.

But he would not have it and said boisterously, "Love to have more Irish arriving into this growing town of ours. Tell me how're you finding Cheyenne and this grand hotel?"

"We've only just arrived," Padraic said, "but the chicken was very well cooked and the spuds were fine."

He held out his hand to Padraic and they shook. "I'm glad to hear that. I think we have one of the finest menus in all of Cheyenne. I'm Tommy Dyer, the owner of this here hotel, and I like to see my guests enjoying themselves."

Then he turned my way and held out his hand to me. I felt his thin but strong hand fold around mine for a moment. "Tommy Dyer, at your service."

We introduced ourselves and he asked from where we came.

"Near Galway," I said.

"Myself, I'm from Dublin, but Molly there comes from close to Galway, too. She's a fine filly, that one."

"So she seems," Padraic agreed.

"What brings you good folks to Cheyenne? Going up to the Black Hills to make your fortune?"

In myself I laughed, thinking we've already done that, but I let Padraic take the answer.

"We've just come from those parts by stagecoach this very day. We're here to check out this town that we've heard so much about."

Tommy Dyer leaned in as if to tell us a secret. "Well, I highly recommend you put down roots. There's land just for the asking. A man can do well for himself."

"That sounds good to me," Padraic said. "We'll have to check into that."

"I'm telling you, it's all up to working hard. Look at me. Came to these parts when I was just nineteen with not a penny, and ten years later I own this hotel. No, this town is definitely on the up and up. We're about to

build an opera house and bring in all the big names direct from the the-
aters in New York."

"That sounds grand," Padraic assured him. "Grand indeed. We're glad
to be here if it's as you say."

I had to break in. I was not forgetting why we were here for one moment. Since Dyer seemed to know so much about what was going on, I
hoped that he might know something of my brother. "We're also here
looking for someone. Maybe you might have heard of him."

Dyer assured me, "If he's Irish, it's most likely I have. I know most all
of them. And there's a slew. Many of them came with the railroad and now
are staying to become fine citizens of this town."

Afraid he was going to launch into another monologue about the
good points of Cheyenne, I interrupted, "His name is Seamus. He's nearly
twenty, and he has red hair the color of a carrot."

He tapped his chin, thinking. "I know a couple Seamuses, but none
that fits that description. Sorry."

"His last name is Reardon. He's my brother." I hoped that saying our
last name might help, as I wondered if Seamus might have changed his
name in an effort not to be found.

"Reardon. Seamus Reardon, red hair." He paused, tapping his lip, then
his eyes lit up. "Oh yes, you'll be meaning Jimmy Reardon."

"Jimmy?" I repeated. But, of course—Seamus was Irish for James, and
Jimmy was a nickname.

"That's what he's called around here. Many of the Irish drop their old
names in favor of a new, more American name. I have had the pleasure of
meeting him a few times. He's quite a dashing young cowboy."

"Cowboy?" I asked.

"Yes, he's signed up with Albert Bothwell, one of the biggest ranchers
in the territory."

The name stopped me. Dyer must be talking of the man I had met on
the street. "So we could find him at this ranch?"

"As far as I know. Haven't seen the lad around here lately. But that
doesn't mean much. I don't get around but stick pretty close to the hotel,
making sure everything's running smoothly."

"And Bothwell's?" Padraic asked. "Where might that be?"

"Oh, sure, I can tell you how to get to Bothwell's. It's not far out of town. A big spread. Anyone hereabouts would know the place and the name. He's one of the richest cattle barons around."

"A big sugar," I murmured to myself.

"Yes, he is that and all," said Dyer. "You've heard of him then?"

"I think I might have met him," I said, remembering how he had addressed me outside the Cheyenne Club. But I pushed that thought away and thought of Seamus. Warmth filled me as I took a long sip of my wine. My dear brother. I would see him soon. Maybe even tomorrow. I could hardly stand to wait. Even though it had only been a short while since I saw him last, I had wondered during that time if I'd ever seen him again, my only relative in this wide country.

"Jimmy." I tried the name in my mouth and shook my head at the feel of it.

4

When we got to our room both of us were too tired to make a fuss over how we would handle our sleeping arrangements. Without having to be told, Padraic waited out in the hall while I slipped out of my dress and pulled on a voluminous nightgown. I had sewn it from a flannel sheet before we left Deadwood, knowing I would need a warm garb on our travels.

When I was settled under the covers, I called out to him. He came in and stripped down to his undershirt and shorts. Unbeknown to him, from the cave of my sheets, I watched him ready himself for bed. In the soft candlelight I saw how lean he was and how his muscles hugged his bones like they were carved. He slid under the covers, wished me a good sleep, "*Codlach samh,*" and lay still in his bed.

When he had settled, I whispered my prayers and prayed for Padraic too, knowing he might not have the energy or the inclination to do so for himself. I took a few moments to enjoy the crisp cleanliness of the sheets, the uncurling of my body in the warmth of the blankets, then I too fell asleep as one dead.

❉   ❉   ❉

When I woke I saw that the sun was already full up in the sky. At first a strange sense of being lost filled me, but when I rolled over and saw Padraic in the next bed, I remembered it all—our trip, our dinner, our quest. I could hear footsteps moving down the hall outside our door in Dyer's Hotel. I knew where I was and what we were to do that busy day.

Sleeping so close to someone in the same room took me back to my home in Ireland, where Mam and Da and the rest of the kids would all sleep in the same room, really the one room we had. I missed it all, I did, but I was where I was and I'd have to make the best of it, starting on this very day.

Now in the bright morning light, I watched Padraic snake out a hand from his bed and grab his trousers and shirt. He sat up and slid into them in one fell swoop. Without turning to look at me, he tiptoed to the door and let himself out. I thought of saying something, but he was so intent on not waking me that it would spoil it to let him know I was already awake. I stretched all the bones in my body. I was alive in this new day, and I had to wonder what it would bring us. Might it be easy to find my brother, get our money, find a place to settle? I so wanted some calm in my life. I whispered to myself, "May we arise with God the Father, Mother Mary, and Saint Patrick. He who saw us safely through this night, may He give us the help and guidance we need to make it safely through this day."

Throwing back the covers, I hurriedly dressed myself, knowing this was the day we were to claim our money. We had been living on the proceeds from selling the house in Deadwood, but those wouldn't keep us going much longer. We had decided to put much of it into a bank, and this felt like real security to me, something I had little experienced in my life. To not have to worry every day about where the money for food was coming from seemed like a grand thing.

I dressed quickly, and when Padraic didn't return within a short time, I went down the stairs to look for him in the dining room.

I found him, but he wasn't alone. Molly was hanging over the next chair, talking and laughing with him. We had slept so late that the dining room was almost empty. I supposed she wouldn't get in trouble for talking to one of the few customers. But I curtly gave my request for biscuits and jam and bacon with coffee and sent her off to fill my order.

"I was after asking her about this Bothwell fellow. Seems he's some sort of bigwig around here. Claims to be the richest rancher in the territory. If that's so, then it sounds like Seamus has landed with a good employer."

"Or not. Just because he's the richest, who knows how he treats his people? He might be a tyrant."

Padraic gave me a look. "What's with you this fine morning? Looking at the dark side of things."

"Nothing. I just want to find my brother."

"And find him we will. But, Brigid, can't you enjoy where we are right now, eating a fine breakfast?"

"Oh, and what makes you so cheery?"

"A good food, a decent sleep, and money forthcoming."

I did not add, "And a young girl hanging on your every word." I only said, "I guess you're right about that."

* * *

We easily found the Western Union office and before going in Padraic danced a little jig and reminded me of his former partner, Billy, one of the finest dancers I had ever had the privilege to dance with. Billy had fallen down a dark hole in the Black Hills and died.

"Time for dancing after we have the money in hand." I prodded him through the doorway. "And then to the bank."

"Yes, I've been recommended to go to the Stockgrowers Bank."

"By whom? I hope not that little waitress," I said and was surprised to hear the tone of jealousy in my voice.

He lifted an eyebrow at me. "No, as a matter of fact, I asked our kind host, Mr. Tom Dyer himself."

"Oh, that was a good idea."

"I'm so glad you approve."

I didn't answer. Padraic seemed a little too full of himself this day, as if he owned it all. I just wanted to get this transaction done and our money safely tucked away in a bank, with some coins of it in our pockets. Then we could go and find my brother.

I waited outside the office, letting Padraic take on this chore himself. Sometimes things went better when it's just the men doing the transaction, but he had promised that my name would be on everything, and I would hold him to that.

I watched the people saunter by, not many women on the streets but lots of men, mainly ranch hands. I couldn't help remarking that the cowboys in Cheyenne were a somewhat different breed of men from the miners in Deadwood. The miners had been dirtier and shuffled along, whereas the cowboys walked tall and took somewhat better care of their attire. I wondered if it had to do with their work; the miners were always stooped over, looking for a glint in the muck, while the cowboys rode out free, heads up high, scanning the horizon.

I decided that I preferred cowboys and wondered how my brother would have taken to his new occupation, if it would have changed him mightily. I still couldn't get over his new name, but the new nickname made sense. And just because he claimed it didn't mean I had to call him that.

Suddenly Padraic burst out the door, and it was not happiness that I saw on his face but anger.

"What now?" I asked, afraid to hear the answer. "It's not there?"

"No, it's there all right. But they won't give it to me."

"What? Isn't your name on it and all?"

"Yes, but since Seamus's name was on the original lease, Mr. Hunt also put your brother's name on the agreement, Seamus Reardon, and they say they can't release the money to me without his signature too."

"Why, that sly man. He knew there was a chance we'd never find him, then we'd never get the money. How could he be so mean about it? I'd like to give him a bit of my tongue."

"I think you already have, Brigid, as I recall."

"Well, this just means we have even more reason to track that brother of mine down and do right quickly." I looked at Padraic and said, "But I was so looking forward to getting you some pants."

"We still have some cash, and I think new pants and maybe a thing or two for you would be a good idea."

❋ ❋ ❋

Not far down Carey Street was the Union Mercantile. I steered Padraic there. We entered and found it a well-stocked store, doing a brisk trade. I persuaded him to buy a pair of wool trousers and let him (because I knew he really wanted it) buy a handsome felt broad-brimmed hat, which he immediately put on, and I swear he grew a couple of inches.

"Should we mosey on over to the Bothwell ranch? See if we can track down that dear brother of yours before he vamooses?" he said in what he must have thought was cowboy slang.

I laughed and gave it back to him, saying in my best American accent, "If you say so, you big galoot."

"Don't you want to go shopping for some clothes for you?" He looked around the store. "I bet they have some pretty dresses here."

"Not now. And not with you. That's something it's best I do on my own."

5

At the livery stable down the street from the hotel, we were able to hire a carriage to drive us out to the Bothwell ranch. I made Padraic remove his new hat when he was seated next to me, as it blocked my view. Also, while these cowboys might wear their hats all day, only taking them off to sleep, I still thought it more proper to take it off when inside a building or carriage.

The ranch road was just beyond the boundaries of the town, and the Bothwell homestead was marked by tall pine logs with a sign claiming it was the way to the Bothwell Ranch, with horseshoes on either side of his name. As Mr. Dyer promised us, the ranch was not to be missed. When the carriage pulled up to the house, we asked the driver to wait for us. He nodded and leaned against the posts as we walked toward the house.

The ranch house was a long structure with only one story, all made of pine logs. At one end was a large carriage house. A barn was a ways down with a corral attached to it. The walkway was stone, and there were large slate flagstones in front of the door. As we walked up I could hear a dog barking inside.

A woman answered the door, wiping her hands on her apron. She looked harried, and I guessed she was in the process of cooking dinner. When we asked for Mr. Bothwell, she pointed in the direction of the barn. "Out yonder. In the pens. They're trying to break a wild one."

Knowing full well what it could mean to "break" a horse, I wasn't looking forward to what we might find. As we walked past the two-story red barn, a piercing squeal cracked the air and stopped me in my tracks. Padraic pulled me forward.

The scene we came upon was sheer mayhem: a golden horse whirling about in the dust with a crew of men shouting and swearing at it. The horse broke free and ran toward us as if it were going to slam right through the bars of the corral, but it stopped and reared back, its eyes white with fear. The scream it let out this time was so close and piercing it hurt my ears with the force of it.

"Make them stop!" I shouted at Padraic.

The horse turned and the men hurled ropes around its neck, a couple of them finding their goal, and they pulled the horse off its feet. Quickly, one man ran in and wrapped a rope around one of its front legs and when it tried to regain its feet, he pulled it down again. As he approached the horse, the beast flailed and kicked him in the shoulder. The way it was thrashing I was afraid it would break its neck. The man tried to get in close to put the rope around its other leg, but the horse was having none of it, so the man then scrambled out of range, jumping the fence. For a moment, the horse lay quite still, its sides shuddering. I could see it was a young and healthy palomino mustang, probably wild from the plains.

"Cussed mustangs," he said, walking toward us. "They're not worth much, even if you can tame 'em. Even these mares."

"Well, that's because you're not going about it the right way," I told him. "You're scaring her to death."

He slapped his hat on his trousers and looked at me. "What do you know about it?"

"Everything my father taught me. And he was a whisperer—he would have them follow him around like a puppy."

"Well, I'd like to see you try to break this one. She's hell on wheels."

A well-dressed gentleman with silver hair and goatee walked around from the other side of the corral. Albert Bothwell himself. He shouted, "That's enough. Leave the horse be. Get those ropes off of her. You clods can't tame the beast that way."

As he walked toward the corral, I told Padraic that he was the man I had talked to when we first arrived in Cheyenne. I mentioned that it was Mr. Bothwell who had told me about the Cheyenne Club.

"What seems to be the matter?" he asked the dusty cowpoke.

"Dang if I know how to break that one. She's nasty as they come. This is the third day and we're getting nowhere. We're never going to get the wild out of her. Is she worth it? Someone's going to get hurt and I don't want it to be me."

"Leave her be for now. Just put her in a stall and give her no food for a day. That'll calm her down."

I couldn't help myself. I couldn't stand how the cowboys were literally trying to break this horse. The words rushed out of me without me wishing them to. "That's not the way to treat a horse. Feed her, but out of your hand. Teach her to trust you."

Bothwell turned toward me as if seeing me for the first time. Then he squinted at me and asked, "Who are you? Do I know you?"

I held out my hand. "I believe you are Mr. Bothwell, and we met by the stagecoach station. Just yesterday."

A smile came to his face and he took my hand. "Ah, yes. You were sitting in the middle of the walkway and wondered about our club. But whatever are you doing here, interfering with my men?"

Padraic stepped forward. "Sir, we're here to ask about someone. A man by the name of Jimmy Reardon. Does he work for you?"

"Jimmy? Yeah, he's one of my new hands. What about him?"

I was glad to hear this news, that we were at the right place. "He's my brother. But he doesn't know I'm here. I haven't seen him in a long while."

"He's not around just now. He's gone out on the range to brand the newborn calves before someone else nabs them."

I knew about branding: cowboys burned marks into the flanks of the animals to show ownership. "When will he be back?"

"Hard to say, little miss."

I wasn't appreciating his way of talking to me, like I was a servant girl or worse. "Your best guess," I said.

"A week or two."

My heart sank. "Can you give him a message when he returns, please? Tell him his sister is at Dyer's Hotel, and if we're not still there, they'll know where to find us."

"I'll surely do that for you. I assume you're a Reardon, too."

"Yes, Brigid Reardon is my name, if you don't remember."

"I won't forget this time, Miss Reardon." He gave a slight bow and walked back toward the house.

"I don't care for that man," I told Padraic.

"If he wasn't your brother's boss, I might have said a thing or two to him." Padraic pounded a fist into his other hand. "Some gentleman. He's got a lot of gall talking to you like that."

"Don't carry on. We've no need to have anything to do with him once Seamus returns." My shoulders sagged along with my spirit. We had found my brother only for him to be impossibly far away with no certain time coming back. I had so hoped to have him in my arms this day.

I turned and saw the golden mustang rise up in the dust of the corral and shake herself off. I felt sorry for her and, like her, felt a bit broken myself. I walked toward the corral and leaned on the fence and put out my hand. The palomino eyed me, then nickered. I started to hum an old tune that my father taught me to quiet the horses who tamed for their masters.

The horse's ears pricked up and she nickered again. I started to sing the words, soft and low. "*Ta me 'mo shui . . .*" The words pulled the horse toward me. I kept singing, luring it to come to me to hear the song better. Slowly, step by careful step, the creature came across the paddock. She got close enough to me that I could see the wild in her but also the wanting of some comfort, as we all do.

At the end of the song, the horse was only an arm's length away, but I didn't try to touch it. I knew, given time, she would have come to me. To have such a horse would be an honor and a gift. She shook out her mane and pawed the ground.

In Gaelic I sang again, "Sweet one, I wish you were a sweet horse of mine."

As we were walking past the barn I heard a sorrowful howl, like a banshee promising no good. What could it be? I wondered. To hear such a sound made me shiver in the heat of the day. The sound was almost like a woman whose heart has broken, but higher and thinner. I knew it must be an animal, but certainly not one I had ever heard before.

6

The hat sitting on my head looked like a confection, something one would want to take a large bite of, covered as it was with fine lace and feathers. Looking in the mirror at myself I couldn't help making a face. But I stifled my laugh, for Mrs. Rose, the saleswoman standing next to me, was starched and very serious about this affair. She had suggested I try it on.

"I don't think so," I said gently as I lifted the hat off, holding it carefully, afraid it might simply float away.

Mrs. Rose gave me rather a stern look. I had the happy thought of turning around and putting the hat on her head. Maybe it would cheer her up, put a smile on her face. But I resisted. "I need something much more practical that I can wear when I'm working outside or horseback riding. More like what the cowboys wear with a brim large enough to keep the sun off my face."

"I'd say it's too late for your face with all your freckles."

I decided she was simply not a nice woman, but I chose not to take her last comment personally. My mother had always told me that freckles were angel kisses, and so I was proud of the ones I had. "Might you show me something a little sturdier, something one might use for everyday?"

She went into the back room and came back with a canvas hat with horsehair trim and a wide brim. When I put it on and looked at myself in the glass, I liked how it became me. It sat well on my head and made me look like I could ride out with the best of them.

"Oh, yes," I said. "This is more what I was looking for."

"But that's for wearing out in the country. You can't be wearing a hat like that in a town like Cheyenne."

"Yes, I think you're right. Show me something simpler than the first one but still somewhat elegant."

She harrumphed and went on her way. When she returned she had a simple straw hat with a silk band and one pheasant feather sticking out back. It reminded me of a Robin Hood hat, rather dashing. When I put it on it made me look like I was someone who loved adventure.

"Oh, yes, this is what I was thinking of. Thank you."

Her face cracked a slight smile. "Would Madam like these both wrapped or perhaps you would like to wear the one on your head?"

"Yes, I think I will wear this one. It fits me so perfectly." Then I turned to her and said, as if trying to explain my lack of hats, "I'm new in town and just trying to find my way around."

The thin, brittle woman stared at me as if waiting for me to say more. Then she asked, "You do seem like a newcomer. But we get lots of those. What brought you to Cheyenne, then?"

"My brother has found work at Albert Bothwell's ranch, and I came out to join him."

She harrumphed. "He's one of our finest ranchers, but I'm not sure I'd want to work for him. I think he's mighty particular. You gotta watch your step around that man."

"How so?"

"Bothwell has been known for taking what isn't his. That's all and more than I should say."

"Thank you for your warning. I might agree with you. The times I've met him I haven't gotten the best impression. He was having a horse broke when we went out there, and I was worried the horse's spirit would be crushed. But maybe that's how they do things around here."

"Well, horses are one thing, but how about those wolves?" she asked as she wrapped my felt hat in tissue and then found a round hatbox. She gently settled it in the box. The hat looked like a fat hen swaddled in a nest.

"Wolves?" I asked.

"Yes, they say he keeps wolves as pets. Keeps them penned up behind the stables. What kind of man would do that? Those animals are good for nothing, but still. They should be shot or set free. That's no life for them."

At her words I remembered the howl that split the air as we were leaving. "I think I heard them when I was out at his ranch. They have a fearful cry, and I'm sure they can be dangerous. But I agree with you that they shouldn't be penned up."

✻ ✻ ✻

I had left Padraic happily ensconced at the hotel bar with a beer. He had insisted that I go out and buy a few things for myself. "We've got enough money to live on for a month or two. Your brother will show up before then. If I can get a new pair of pants and this fine hat, then you should be able to buy a few things you need."

This style of shopping was all a new experience for me—to go into a store and feel like I didn't need to penny-pinch. I had to keep reminding myself that the coming money was what I had earned as clearly as Seamus and Padraic had done. I had negotiated the payment of our mine in the Black Hills—and had driven a hard bargain at that.

Having thought about it for a while (ever since I knew we would be coming into some money), I had made a mental list of exactly what I wanted to buy. Besides a new hat or two, I needed a new pair of boots and some yarn to knit myself a shawl; the one I had made last year was wearing thin. That would be good for a start. Oh, and possibly fabric for a new dress, if it wasn't too dear. Also, I'd love to buy a book or two, but so far I hadn't seen any sort of bookstore.

✻ ✻ ✻

Mrs. Rose had recommended that I go to Smith and Harrington for the best selection of boots and fabric. I walked the few blocks to the store and was pleased to see a sign in the window that read, "New Shipment of Shoes and Boots, Fresh from Chicago."

When I walked in I was greeted by a woman who ushered me to the footwear department. After measuring my foot, she offered me a pair of lovely brown boots with hooks up the side. The saleswoman slid one on my foot and it felt like a slipper, so comfortable it was.

"My, that's a lovely thing," I said, looking down at the handsome boot.

"It's the latest style from out East," the saleswoman said as she slipped the other boot on my other foot.

"But not too dainty," I said, standing up and walking around. "I need to be able to hike around in them."

"These should serve you well."

"You also sell fabric and yarn here?" I asked.

"Yes, that's another department. I'll fetch someone to wait on you."

After I took off the boots and she wrapped them up for me, she went to get someone. A small and dapper salesman followed her and took me to where the fabrics were shelved. "We just got a new shipment of calico. Are you a seamstress?" he asked as he led me to a pile of bolts of fabric.

"I can sew a simple seam—enough to make a plain dress, I think." Then I couldn't help myself, and I reached out my hand and ran it down the fabric just to feel the newness of it. There was a lovely brown-flowered calico that spoke to me. I could see an easy housedress made of that.

Without thinking I said, "I'll take three yards of that brown piece."

"Very good, Madam." He handed the bolt of fabric to a young girl to cut it for me.

"And I'd like some yarn for an everyday shawl."

He led me to the racks of yarn. "I'd suggest this brown wool to go with your fabric."

When he handed it to me, I could almost smell the heather in it. The wool reminded me so much of the Irish sheep. "Perfect."

He smiled at my delight. "You are Irish, are you not?" he asked.

"Yes, indeed," I said, hoping he wouldn't put me down for my heritage. Some of the words they called us Irish were not for anyone's ears.

But instead he smiled and said, "Then you know good wool."

"Yes, I think I do."

"May I show you the new wool tweed that has just come from Magee's of Donegal?"

"Of course." I knew the name but never thought I would have the wherewithal to buy any of their goods. The wool fabric he rolled out before me was flecked, as were the hills and valleys of my homeland, with bits of color like flowers in a field. I ran my hand over the thick fabric and knew it to be good.

"My, but this is wonderful." Then I saw a piece tucked behind the first that I liked even better. It was a deep, dark green with blue flecks. I pointed it out to him. "Could I see that wool?"

"We've sold most of that bolt to Mr. Bothwell. I think he is having a suitcoat made of it and needed quite a lot of fabric."

Once again this man's name had come up. "That man surely gets around. My brother is his employee."

"Yes, he is one of the largest land barons and somewhat notorious in these parts. Mr. Bothwell is a very good customer of ours." He stopped himself, then added, "I will say no more than that."

While I wondered what more he might have to say, I decided to honor his decision. "It looks that you don't have much of that fabric left."

He held up what looked to be a bit more than a yard. "Enough I would say for a vest. Perhaps for your brother?" he suggested.

He had guessed right. From the moment I had seen the color of the fabric, I had seen Padraic, my pretend brother, in it. "I'll take what remains."

He then helped me buy what I would need—needles and pins and thread—to sew the dress and vest. After my pile was assembled, he handed me several lead bars, shaped like lozenges. I looked at them in surprise.

"You'll need these," he told me.

"Whatever for?" I could feel the weight of them and couldn't imagine what I would do with them.

"The wind here is fierce. It can take a dress like you'll be making and throw it right over your head. To safeguard themselves, women sew these into the hems at the bottoms of their dresses. I thought you might not know this."

"I surely didn't."

For the shawl I told him I already had knitting needles of my own; my father had whittled them for me. I thought how good it would be to have them in my hands once again. And this fine wool was certainly a step up from the ratty yarn I had used to make my last shawl.

The small man carefully folded and piled up my purchases. "Excellent choices, Madam. And may I have these delivered to where you are staying?"

I had a moment of feeling like the grand lady I wasn't, but maybe I could learn to be. To have packages delivered was certainly a nice feature.

I nodded as if I did this sort of thing all the time. "Yes, that would be fine. We're at Dyer's Hotel."

"A fine Irish establishment," he said as he walked me to the door of the store. "I often send customers there who are visiting our fair city."

"Thank you for all your help. I will certainly stop in again," I promised him and was sure I would.

He smiled and it changed him into a much more charming man. "I hope you are happy with all your purchases and that we have the pleasure of seeing you again very soon. You might stop in and show me your new dress when you have finished it. Be sure to use those weights."

I thought of one more thing I needed. "Might you tell me where there is a bookstore?"

He smiled and nodded. "But of course. Not far from here. Just down on Ferguson Street you'll find Mr. William Masi's establishment. He carries a fine selection of books and stationery."

I thanked him, and he opened the door for me. I stepped out onto the sidewalk. Then the world erupted around me.

7

I had been warned that the streets of Cheyenne could be a somewhat dangerous place, but I had assumed that the brawling took place at night—after the drinking and gambling had started—and I didn't plan to be awake for it. Here it was, the middle of the day, and a scuffle had broken out that included horses rearing and lunging, guns being shot into the air, and screams from the ladies and swearing from the men.

I backed into the doorway of the mercantile but stayed outside to watch the commotion. As far as I could make out, two men on horseback were trying to ride a slender young man down, shooting their pistols in the air as they did so. He was running away as fast as he could, but they had him cornered. Finally, one of them grabbed him by the scruff of his shirt and flung him to the ground. The other turned his horse on its heels and came near to trampling the man. The slender man landed on his back, not far from where I was standing, and I saw in fact that he was young. He was just a lad. Younger than I was, maybe fifteen at the most. In his effort to get off the street and out of danger, he scrabbled and pushed with his boots, hanging on to his hat as he did so. Just as he had reached the sidewalk right in front of me and was hoisting himself up, one of the men rode by on his horse. The man was wearing a large hat with feathers tucked in the brim. Half his face was covered with a dark red beard and he was laughing. As he wheeled and turned, he came closer and shot at the lad.

The sound was like a roar and an explosion. I couldn't help but cover my ears and shut my eyes for a moment. When I opened them, things were quieting down—the two men on horseback broke into a gallop, heading down the street away from town. The poor lad lying on the street was holding his leg and whimpering. He sounded like an animal, his piteous cries close to the mewling of a newborn.

I stepped out of the doorway and walked to where he was, bending over to see if I could help. His face was squinched in pain and his mouth was wide open but without any sound coming out, until he saw me and cried out, "Help me, please, help! I think they shot off my foot."

Unfortunately, I saw that he was close to right. Where his boot used to be was a ball of gory matter with a shoelace sticking out, blood pooling on the street. Not knowing what to do, I put my hand on his forehead and tilted his head back so he couldn't see the damage the bullet had done.

I told him, "It will be all right," knowing full well it wouldn't and might never be all right.

He calmed down a bit and stared at me. "You think so?"

"Why were they after you?" I had to ask, avoiding his question.

"I took a blanket last night. I was cold so I borrowed their blanket. That's all. They shot me 'cuz of a blanket."

I shook my head. This town was not to be believed. To shoot a man over a borrowed blanket. It made me feel crazy to even be in such a place where a thing like this could happen.

A man ran over to us, carrying a large black Gladstone bag. "I'm a doctor. I'll take over from here." He pushed me out of the way and immediately wrapped a tourniquet around the boy's leg.

"Will you be able to fix his foot?" I stood over him, watching.

The doctor, a man in his late fifties I guessed, shook his head and stood to talk to me. He wiped his hands on his pants. "Idjit sons o' bitches. No way to say until I see it better. I've got to get him in my office." Two men walked over then, and between the three of them they hoisted the injured boy, using their arms to make a sling under him. The boy's face turned ashen and he slumped into their arms. A pool of blood was left behind on the dirt street, but soon it would be covered in the dust.

I watched them carry him across the street and down the block to what I assumed was the doctor's office. I couldn't help thinking that it would be hard to be any kind of cowboy with only one foot and him so young.

"What happened?" a blowsy woman who had come next to me asked. She looked down and saw the blood in the street. "I heard the noise. Did someone get shot again?"

"Yes, and can you believe it—the fight was over a blanket."

She laughed a coarse, hard laugh. She was a large woman wearing a calico dress that fit her like it was made for someone much smaller, revealing far too much of her ample chest. "I heard tell once of a cowpoke shooting someone simply because he was snoring. Not that I haven't thought of doing such a thing myself to my own husband, once in a moon."

"How does one protect oneself in this town with all this gunfire around?" I asked her. After what had happened in Deadwood, I had hoped to find less violence in this new town.

"You get used to it. They're usually not shooting at us women, that's a promise. But it's best to steer clear of the stray bullets." She looked me up and down. "You're new here, then?"

"Yes, this is only my second day in town. We came down from Deadwood on the coach."

"You plan on staying in town?" Again, she gave me a careful looking over. "A fine-looking girl like you could find work here no trouble at all. The saloons are always needing more fancy ladies."

"I doubt I'd do that, but I would like to do something. It all depends on my brother Seamus. He's a cowboy on a ranch outside town."

"Well, then you might think about going out to the range and homesteading a piece for yourself."

"Homesteading? I've not really considered that," I said. "I don't think we know what we're going to do."

"Well, you should think about it. It's the time to do it."

"How does one go about getting a homestead?"

"It's easy as pie." She laughed. "Even women can claim one—those women trying to get the vote seen to that. I've even thought of it. They're just about giving the land away. Can't do much better than that."

"Thank you. It certainly is something to think about." The fact that I could actually own land myself had never occurred to me. Wouldn't that make my father proud? He always said that land made a man rich.

8

The horror of what I'd witnessed rose up in me until I thought I would be sick with it. I had to find Padraic and tell him what had happened. I needed to talk to someone, and he had to know of such things. A foot shot off right in front of me. A young lad maimed for life. The needless destruction of it. I tried not to think as I ran back to our hotel. How could people behave that way? I wondered, breathless from the sadness of it. Something deep within me gave way as if the world was more cruel than I had ever imagined.

I hurried through the entryway of the hotel, then looked over to the bar, where I had left Padraic, and I saw he was still there. Thank God. But as I rushed to talk to him, I also saw that he was not alone. Our waitress of last night, Molly, was sitting next to him on a bar stool, as pretty as you please, and they were sharing a laugh.

A laugh, from stern-faced Padraic? As I watched, she brushed her hand against his shoulder in a very welcoming way. I did not like what I was seeing. I stopped a few feet away, not sure if I should break up their little tête-à-tête. They looked so carefree. Who was I to ruin that and bring bad news to them?

Molly was dressed in an outfit that seemed more appropriate for an afternoon tea than a drink in a bar. With a fine crinoline skirt, mutton-sleeved blouse, and her hair up in a chignon with curls around her face, she could have sat for a *carte de visite*. Padraic had his new hat pushed back on his head and looked as relaxed as I'd ever seen him. I hoped it was the drink and not the company that made him feel happy.

But then Molly saw me and motioned me over. "We were wondering when you'd be back."

Padraic turned and stood up from his bar stool. "There she is, herself. Where are all the goods?"

"They're being delivered," I managed to say.

Molly said, as if an explanation of why they were laughing, "Paddy was just telling me about your stagecoach ride here. They go over some mighty rough terrain coming down from the Black Hills."

"You can say that again," I agreed.

"How'd your shopping trip go?" Padraic asked.

"Fine, I guess." I heard my voice waver. I could hardly speak. How to start with my story?

"Well, come join us for a drink. Molly has the afternoon off, and we're reminiscing about the old country. She's got some tales to tell about how she came to be here." He pulled his eyes away from Molly and finally looked at me. I bowed my head, not wanting to meet his eyes.

He looked at me closely. "What's the matter, Brigid? Did something happen to you?"

"Yes, you could say that. There was after a terrible shooting just down the street. I had only stepped outside—" I broke off as my voice started to quaver and I grew angry at what I had seen.

Padraic put out his hand to pull me closer. "Just now? Where? Are you all right, then?"

At his question I felt myself tremble, remembering. "Not really. It was awful to see. Two cowboys ran this poor lad down in the street. He fell at my feet and then—" I couldn't go on.

Molly waved a hand. "The cowboys are always tearing up the place. Goes on here all the time."

I continued, looking at Padraic. "But this was more. One of them shot him. The blow took his foot off. He was right in front of me and there was blood everywhere, and I tried to help and told him it was going to be all right, even when I knew—" I could no longer keep back the tears and my anger. "How could they do that? What is the matter with those men? What kind of place is this?"

"Oh, *macushla*. Hush now." Padraic pulled me into his arms.

I squirmed a bit, not sure I wanted his comfort, but then I gave in and sank into his arms. Molly turned away as if she was witness to something she didn't want to see. She would know what the Irish word *macushla* meant, that Padraic had called me "his heart." In a way I hated to have her see me like this—I felt so vulnerable—but my angry tears kept coming no matter how hard I tried to pull them back. Padraic handed me a bandanna.

"Where was this?" Padraic asked.

I took a deep breath and blew my nose. "Not far away. Right in front of the mercantile. It was a blessing the doctor was only down the street and they hauled the poor lad away to his office. But I'm afraid the truth is he's in a bad way. There was nothing much left of his foot."

I stared at Padraic. "How could those men do that? And the fight was over a blanket."

"A blanket?" He just shook his head. "I know what you need." Padraic turned to the bartender and said, "Let's have a shot of your finest whiskey."

A small glass of the golden liquor was put on the counter. Padraic reached for it and handed it to me. "Drink up, Brigid. You need something to settle you down. This will do the trick."

I had little taste for hard liquor but forced myself to take a large sip of the whiskey. It burned, then warmed, but I still felt cold inside. I tried to keep out the image of the blown-apart foot, but it was like a burning sun shining through everything. I swallowed the rest of the whiskey, hoping it would make me forget.

Molly stood and said to Padraic, "Thanks for the beer. It was nice to talk to you. I've got to get ready for work."

"Thanks for your company." He stood and gave her a slight bow.

"See you later?" she asked.

"We'll be down for dinner," he answered.

As Molly was leaving she turned and said to me, "Sorry you had to see such a thing, but you'll get used to the ganging around and shooting if you stick around this town. After all, it's the frontier."

"I do not look forward to getting accustomed to such violence," I replied. "So maybe we won't be sticking around."

"Well, all I know is this town is not for the faint of heart," she said with a slight smile.

"All I know is there are better ways—and maybe better places—to live." I leaned into Padraic's arms as if to own him.

9

The steak I ordered that night was served to me on a white plate. I stared at it, repulsed. It had sounded good when I saw it on the menu, but red juice oozed out and puddled around it. This piece of meat was now too bloody for me to stomach after what I had seen that day. I pushed the plate away and said, "I'm sorry but I can't eat this. I know I ordered it, but it's just too raw."

Padraic, without saying a word, gave me his meal of stew and took my steak. After a pause he looked at me and said, "I'm sorry you had to see what you did. I should have been with you."

"You couldn't have done a thing. And seeing that poor young boy get his foot shot off all brought back what I had done, Paddy." I tried to explain. "After all, I did close to the same thing in Deadwood. I shot a man. Charlie Hunt was turned away from me, too."

"You did what you had to do to stop him from getting away. It was a brave thing, Brigid."

"Yes, but what is it in this country that brings out the savage in us? In all of us? Even me."

"One must take the good with the bad, I suppose. The open country, the frontier, little sense of law and order. I have no good answer for all your questions. Like you I wonder at the violence of this place. All the guns they carry? What are they so angry about?"

His gentle voice musing over what was bothering me calmed me down, as his words so often did. But I could not forget that in Deadwood I had shot a man in the leg and injured him badly. I was forced to do it to save myself and to keep him from getting away with his crimes, yet the memory haunted me. Even I was capable of violence.

"Maybe it's more that they're scared," I suggested, remembering how I had felt as I pulled the trigger. "Maybe they don't know what else to do."

❀   ❀   ❀

Molly was not our waitress that night, for which I was thankful, but she was working in another part of the dining room. I watched her swish around in her uniform. But she couldn't stay away from our table. She came tripping over almost as soon as we sat down, bringing Padraic a bottle of beer.

"I know what you like so I've brought it to you." She smiled at him as she set down the bottle. "On the house."

"Many thanks," he said. "You're a fine waitress."

"Kind of you to say, Sir." Then she laughed. And Padraic laughed, too. This exchange didn't strike me as that humorous so I kept quiet.

She put a hand on my shoulder and said, "I hope you're doing better after all that happened to you today."

"Thanks, much recovered," I answered curtly.

But she didn't take the hint and turned back to Padraic. "Enjoy your meal. And your beer. The steak looks awfully good tonight. Might have to try it myself." She left us with a twitter.

"She's a cheery lass," Padraic commented.

"Hmm. If you like that sort." I took a bite of the stew and found it warming and hearty.

"I take it you do not care for her," he stated.

"I do not know her," I answered, not wanting to get into the matter with him. It would serve nothing.

"Yes, there's that. But she's been nothing but kind to us since we've arrived. You could use a friend." I did not disagree so I said nothing. "On top of that, she told me how she and others are fighting for the right to vote, and I know how much you admire those women. She could probably introduce you to others of a like mind."

"I suppose," I conceded.

❀   ❀   ❀

When we were finished with our meals, Tommy Dyer, playing the good host, approached our table and asked how our food had been.

"The stew was so comforting, felt like I was home for a bit," I told him. "Although it was better than Ma ever made."

"The steak was done perfectly," Padraic said, giving me a sly look. "Just the way I like it."

"May I join you for a moment?" Dyer asked. Without waiting for an answer, he pulled up a chair and slid in next to us. "I have some news that I thought might be of interest to you." He beamed at us as if he were about to hand us a gift.

"Out with it then," Padraic said. "If it's our interest you want, you have it, Mr. Dyer."

"Well, I don't know what you're all about, but have you considered claiming some land around here?"

"We've thought of it, but we've only just arrived," I said.

"It has more than occurred to me," Padraic said.

I was taken aback by how determined Padraic sounded. We had talked of it as a possibility, but I had my concerns. Here he sounded like he was all ready to do it—but we had to find Seamus before we did anything else.

"Well, an old friend of mine, Irish himself, has made the hard decision to quit his claim." Dyer cleared his throat and continued. "'Tis a sad story. He has two small ones and his wife died giving birth to the last. He's going back East to her family as he cannot raise the two wee ones on his own. So his homestead will be up for grabs. It already has a soddy on it, and I think even a small corral. It would save you much time and money."

"A soddy?" I asked. "You mean like a house built out of sod?"

"Sure and that's it. A turf house we would call it. You know, with so little timber available on the prairie it's a good way to go. Built into the earth, they can be very solid and warm."

"And dirty. Much like the house I left behind," I said quietly, thinking of the animals that had lived with us.

"What would we need to do?" Padraic asked. I could tell by the lilt of his voice that he was interested.

Mr. Dyer explained the process of transferring the deed and told us where we would have to go to settle with his friend. "The homestead is well situated, right out by Clear Creek and with good prairie grass for live-stock. Can't ask for more. And I don't think he's told anyone but me so far."

"We'll have to talk it over," I interrupted.

"Yes, of course." He paused for a moment. "It's just, I like to see my fellow countrymen settling the land around here. So often we Irish haven't been treated well, but here, in Cheyenne, we're staking our claims and be-coming respected."

Padraic nodded at that. "So it would seem."

"Why, look at me." Mr. Dyer slapped himself on his chest. "As I told you I had to make my way alone. Came when the railroad was coming through and bought this old place. Don't say I haven't worked hard, but this," he stretched his arms out to take in the room, "is my reward."

He looked pretty pleased with himself, and I thought he had a right to be.

"You've certainly set a good example for the rest of us," I told him.

Then he added, "And, of course, I have my lovely wife and children. If you're willing to work, you can make something of yourself unlike in the old country, where we couldn't even own the land we worked. The damn English saw to that." I loved hearing again the story of his success—it gave me such hope. Yes, the frontier was wild and sometimes ruthless, but there was room to move and grow and succeed. There was that.

"Yours is indeed a remarkable tale. One that is heard fair often in this vast country," I said.

"Aye," he said, "but a story that is even more remarkable is of the fine gentleman who owns the Intercontinental Hotel down the street."

"Do tell," I urged. I had seen this hotel in passing, and it was said to be the finest establishment this side of the Mississippi River.

"Barney Ford is his name, the owner of the hotel. He started life in Virginia as a slave."

Dyer must have seen the look on my face because he said, "Yes, that's right. His father was the plantation owner and his mother was a slave. Taught himself to read and write and headed west. Built a hotel in Denver, which was so popular he came here in 1870 and built another one. Talk about making the most of yourself. That man puts the rest of us to shame."

"Why, how did he ever do that?" I couldn't help wondering at the determination of such a man.

"Start small and grow. That's the name of the game in this land," Mr. Dyer said philosophically.

Padraic nodded. "My father, bless his soul, always wanted a bit of turf. But 'twas not to be, as you have said. Just not possible in Ireland. But here in this country it's a different story."

Mr. Dyer stood and pushed in his chair. "Well, think on it, but don't be slow. Else someone else might jump in front of you."

"Thanks for the tip," Padraic said.

"Always glad to help a fellow countryman," he said, then turned toward me, "and lady." He smiled as he included me. "May I offer you desserts on the house? We have a nice blancmange."

Not knowing what that dessert was I simply smiled and nodded. "How kind. That would be very delightful."

"Talk over what I've proposed. But if I were you two, I would jump at the chance to grab a claim already established."

After he had left, Padraic turned to me. "Brigid, what a chance, is it not? How can we not do this?"

"I wish Seamus were with us. It's hard for me to think of anything until we're back with him. Plus, the money, which we do not have."

"It might be another month or two before Seamus is back, and Dyer says we daren't wait. Let's see what it might cost—after all, I've heard they're giving away the land for free."

"Well, I'm not sure I can make such a big decision without my brother being in on it."

"I understand, but it's not that big a risk if you think about it. It sounds like the place is ready to move into. We would save the money we're spending here at this hotel. And in a few years' time, we would own it. Our very own house and land. Think of it, Brigid."

"I am thinking."

"This might be our chance, we could have our own place, get some cattle, build it up, and who knows—maybe we would be the next cattle barons."

"Or big sugars, as they call them." I had to smile. The thought of it all was beguiling.

"Let's give it a go, Brigid. We have hardly a thing to lose."

"Wouldn't Seamus be surprised to find us with our own place when he comes back to town?" I laughed at the thought of it.

"Say yes," Padraic insisted.

"I don't see why not if you're so dead set on it."

"That I am."

"Well, then let's find out more about it."

Just then our waiter placed two bowls of white pudding in front of each of us. The whiteness of the pudding made it resemble a jiggling pile of snow. I knew enough French to know that its name meant "white eat." I tasted the dessert and found it was as sweet as milk right from the cow and slippery going down. I sighed after I took another bite. "Delicious."

Padraic was lost in thought. He whispered, while looking across the room as if in a dream, "Our own land."

Part II

The Soddy

I am looking rather seedy now while holding down my claim,
And my victuals are not always served the best;
And the mice play shyly round me as I nestle down to rest
In my little old sod shanty on my claim.
Yet, I rather like the novelty of living in this way,
Though my bill of fare is always rather tame,
But I'm happy as a clam on the land of Uncle Sam
In the little old sod shanty on my claim.

—Cowboy Songs

10

Pushing open the door of the soddy, the smell was what hit me first, dank yet almost sweet, the scent of spoiled things. I hated to think what I might find in the corners of the one-room sod house when I thoroughly explored it.

I ducked my head under the lintel to enter the room farther and was not pleased with what I saw. A pallet in a corner with soiled bedclothes, a broken chair tipped over, a table with a dirty bowl, a mouse scurrying away to some hole. And looking up, I saw that the sheet, which had been hung over the ceiling to keep the dirt from falling into the house, was ripped and falling down. All in all, the place was a right mess.

The soddy was more like a cave than a house. Dark walls, dirt floor, and one window made from one pane of glass. I remembered hearing that for it to be a legitimate house on the homestead it must have a door and a glass window. So this place did, but the door would keep no creature out and the window let little light in.

I closed my eyes for a moment and pulled back my shoulders. All things were possible.

Somehow in my mind I had imagined that we would find it all comfort and cleanliness waiting for us. But how wrong I was. And seeing it now I chided myself. What had I been thinking? The poor man had lost his wife and couldn't handle his children. He cared nothing for how he left the home he had lost. He took what he could and left the rest. At least maybe some of the furniture could be used. I backed out of the place and took a deep breath of clean air. Padraic was surveying the prairie.

I had to admit the land was a fine sight, unlike the dwelling. Even the outside of the house was more comely, as it was dug into a hillside and covered with tall red grasses and yellow flowers. The land was gently rolling with clumps of bushes. Out farther the grass was nearly taller than I could reach. There was a lushness about it all, but I had to remind myself that it was spring with its early bloom and hopefulness.

Another good sight met my eye. Far down the side of the hill was a stream, which I guessed was Clear Creek. I hoped the water would live up to its name. What a help that would be to be able to bathe and swim and drink out of it—at least for the time being.

"Just a bit of paradise," Padraic said. "Don't you agree, my Brigid?"

First of all, I wasn't sure I was his Brigid. And second I felt like I needed to reach out and pull his feet down from the sky, his own happiness had him flying so high. "You've yet to see the house."

"That we can fix," he said. Walking over to me he threw an arm around my shoulders. "But this land is why we've come to America. This is why we're here. Can't you see?"

I leaned into him. "I guess."

Whatever I thought of the soddy, there was no turning back. We had signed the papers, handed over what remained of our money, and received the deed for the homestead. The man who had driven us out in his wagon unloaded our trunks with Padraic's help and then drove away. We had bought a few supplies in town, and I was glad that I had thought to bring a bucket, broom, and soap. Before anything went into the hovel that was to be our home, I would need to sweep and clean it top to bottom.

"The corral looks like it needs only a little work to be put back into shape," Padraic commented.

"That's good, but we've nothing to put in it."

"They will come. Can you not see the good of all this?" he asked, stepping away from me. He looked and sounded disappointed.

"Someone has to be sensible," I snapped back.

"That may be. But there's a time for being sensible and a time for being happy for what we have." He walked away and carried one of the trunks toward the house. "We're moving in."

"Not yet, Padraic. Please. Leave that by the door. I need to do some serious cleaning before the place is fit for our gear."

"I'll help. What can I do?"

"You can take the bucket and go to the creek for water."

"Might be almost warm enough for a swim," he cracked.

"Don't you dare. We will not be sleeping tonight until that place is fit for human habitation."

✳   ✳   ✳

Hours later, after cleaning and repairing what we could, we were beyond tired and hungry. We sat on our trunks at the table that Padraic had repaired and ate bread and cheese and beer.

"We've done what we can today," Padraic said, looking around the room.

"No, there's one more thing. I'm going out to cut grass for the floor. A carpet of grass will cut down on the dirt and make this room smell better."

"The two of us will do it. I'll cut and you can harvest."

Slowly we got up from the table to go to the fields.

The night air smelled of growing and the moon shone like a cup of light in the sky. The birds were singing their good-night songs and the wind was soft and warm. I breathed it all in.

"This blasted thing is almost worthless," Padraic complained as he took the scythe to the grass, but by sheer force he managed to mow down hanks of the tall grass.

I gathered armfuls of this sweet grass and brought them into the soddy, first laying them at the corners and moving inward. As I worked, I regained some of my resolve. This was just a start. I hoped that we would gain better things. A wooden floor would be a godsend, but for now grass would have to do.

There was only one pallet and, of course, Padraic insisted I sleep on it. I mounded up grass for him in the far corner and hoped he would be comfortable on that for the time being.

When we had finished, we were almost out of words with fatigue. Too tired to change out of our clothes, we each took a blanket and went to our beds.

"Brigid?" Padraic's voice floated through the room.

"Yes?"

"Could you give us a prayer?"

Yes, I thought, it was what we both needed. A prayer that would help us settle into this new home.

And so I recited the house blessing my dear father had taught me, which we had said often as we went to bed.

May God bless this house from bottom to top,
May He bless each lintel, each stone, and each board,
May He bless the family and the food-laden table,
May He bless each bed, place of gentle sleep through the night,
May He bless the door open in hospitality
to both strangers and beggars, and to our own kith and kin,
May He bless the windows, letting in all the light—
the bright rays of the sun, the moon, and the stars—
May He bless the walls that rise above our heads,
and again the outer walls, which encircle us today.
May peace, love, and goodwill bless our neighbors.
May God bless this family and keep us out of danger.
May He gather all who live in this house to Himself.

11

When a beam of the early morning sun shone on the new grass of our soddy floor, I opened an eye and shook myself awake. My body was sore from all the cleaning and carrying I had done yesterday. I hadn't worked that hard in quite a while. I looked over at the lump that was Padraic. He was sprawled across the blanket, clutching his grass bed as if he were hugging it. Looking at him, I felt a deep love but was so unsure of what it meant. I was certainly unsure of what he wanted. We needed to talk. There was such a sense of tension between us. Left to our own devices, without my brother around, we didn't know what we were to each other. Maybe tonight over dinner, after our work was done, I'd try to broach the subject.

But what I was really waiting for with all my might was the first sight of my brother. At least we knew where he was and that he would return. I knew I must be satisfied with that. But it was very hard to wait. It felt like I could think of little else and that all the things that I must decide, like was this even the life I wanted, had to wait until he was back.

I shed my blanket and walked into the sunlight of the new day. The bucket lay near the fire we had cooked over last night. I knew which direction the creek was and grabbed the bucket to fetch the water. As my skirts swished through the tall grass, bugs and butterflies flew and sounded around me. I saw a meadowlark holding fast to a tall stalk of grass, singing its head off. Yes, it was a fine day.

The creek was making its own burbling sounds. I squatted at the edge of it and cupped the water in my hands to wash my face. Then I took a long drink. The closeness of the creek made me more sure of what we were doing. Land with water was always more valuable. Who knows, someone might come and offer us a lot more for this land than we had paid for it. I might not be living here forever. The thought lightened me, for I still had thoughts of traveling to a bigger city.

I filled the bucket with the clear water and tried not to let it all slosh out on my trip back to the soddy. As I walked up, I saw that Padraic had risen and was bent over the fire, getting it going again. The ritual of the new day—coffee and bread.

"Thanks for doing that, Brigid."

"No need for thanks. We're in this together."

He laughed. "I guess we are at that. No regrets?"

"I'm not sure I can say that yet."

"Yes, but we've done it."

I made the coffee and he carefully toasted the bread over the fire. He was better at it and didn't burn the pieces as I was known to do. We sat in the brightening sun and ate our breakfast perched on a couple of large rocks.

"I'm going to walk into town," he said.

"Why? Already? We just got here."

"I can see that there's a few things we need right away. No sense waiting. It won't take me long. It's just a couple miles. I'll be back in the afternoon."

I knew enough not to argue with him. He had a better sense than I about what we would need out here. But I too had already made a short list in my head. "Get a ham hock, if you would, and some dried beans. That will keep us going for a few days."

I watched Padraic walk away until he disappeared over the rise. Instead of jumping up to work on the soddy, I sunk to the ground. After a few minutes of feeling very alone, I made myself get up and go back into the darkness of the house. There was still so much cleaning to do. While plumping up and straightening Padraic's bed and blanket, I saw that he had used his jacket for a pillow, and I made my mind up that we would get real pillows soon, with down filling, if they could be found.

I was sitting on the floor and found I barely could bring myself to stand. So I stayed where I was. Padraic and I had been in each other's company for the past many days, and I had had no time to reflect on all that had happened. The rupture of our departure from Deadwood was a wound I tried to keep away from, but still my mind wandered there when I had a moment alone. The good and the bad of it mingled so that I had trouble knowing how I felt about it all—the horrible death of Billy falling into a mine shaft. Somehow it seemed my fault, as if I should have been able to stop or save him.

And then having to defend myself against a man I had come close to loving, even thinking of marrying him. As sure as I was sitting on a pile of grass, I knew that given the chance he would have left me at the mine. While I probably would have survived, someone coming to find me sooner than later, by that time Charlie Hunt would have gotten away, scot free, after he had murdered a woman. I could not let that happen, so I had forced myself to shoot him in the leg. He still got off easy. And then I used that to bargain with his father for more money for our mine. But none of it sat well with me, and even thinking of it now I had to wonder how it could have been different. As often as I told myself not to dwell on it, these thoughts ran through me like a hidden river.

The best thing to do was to keep working on the house. There was so much to do that I barely knew where to start. I could hear my mother saying to me, "Put one foot in front of the other, and before you know it you will be halfway done."

The grass I had laid on the floor last night had dried and shrunk, so I went to gather more. As I was spreading it out, I found a small wooden doll hidden under the table. She had big carved-out eyes and a slash of a grin on her face. The father must have made it for his little girl. The doll fit in the palm of my hand. I felt bad for the girl. She must have dropped it, and then in their hurry they had left it behind. Holding the doll carefully, I sat in our only chair. It wobbled as I shifted my weight. Suddenly it gave way and I fell to the floor, the leg of the chair shooting toward the wall.

The fall jarred me so that my teeth clacked together. The doll flew from my hands and fell into the grass on the floor. I looked around me. Here I was, sitting on the grass of the floor. With barely a thought, tears spurted from my eyes. Looking around the dark and dingy room I started to sob, huge wracking sobs that tore through my heart and up my throat. This was all too much for me. All of it—boys getting their feet shot off, women dying in childbirth, little girls losing their dolls, my brother gone away, no friends, even Padraic gone. I felt like I too had lost everything. I was not where I wanted to be.

In all my dreams of the new country, I never imagined myself sitting crumpled on the floor of a falling-down soddy house. Here I was, right back where I started, sleeping in a hole in the ground, like I had with my family back in Ireland. This thought shocked me into silence. How had this happened? I started to weep more quietly and wrapped my arms around myself. But it was little comfort, and I missed my family and my home more than ever.

A sharp rap came from the doorway.

12

I turned, not knowing what I expected to see. The silhouette of an un-known person filled the doorway. With the sun shining bright behind, I could not make out properly who it might be.

"Howdy," came a deep voice, but one that sounded friendly.

I snuffled, stood up, and wiped at my face. I knew I looked a mess, but I tried to sound fine. "Hello. Please come in."

"I'm in."

I couldn't tell if the soul standing in front of me was a man or a woman. Wearing a large floppy hat, with hair pulled back into a tail, I thought at first a man. But the person was not that tall and, as I could gradually see better, appeared to be wearing some kind of skirt.

A glove came off and a hand shot toward me. "I'm Ella." I took the rough hand and we shook. As she stepped out of the light, I could see that she had a broad, warm face and a wide smile. The floppy hat was in fact a large sunbonnet.

"Live just the other side of that rise. I'm your nearest neighbor. Thought I'd come over and see how you're making out."

"That's kind of you. I'm Brigid. As you can see we're in the midst of getting settled here."

"Yup, I was sorry to hear about the troubles of Mr. Sullivan. Mind you, he didn't have the sense that God gave geese, but he wasn't a bad sort. Good enough neighbor when it came to that."

"Yes, his is a sad story. I feel so badly for his poor children."

"Speaking of poor, I couldn't help hearing you were having a bit of a cry in here," she said, looking down at the floor. "Not that it never happens to me. Just a bit of too much around here?"

"Would you like to sit down?" I pointed to one of our trunks. I seated myself on the other. "Our one chair just broke and landed me on the floor."

"It's a tough reckoning, setting up a place like this," she said, trying to get comfortable on her seat. "I've taken it into my head to cry a few times. So don't feel bad about that."

"I just . . . I just don't know where to start," I stammered.

"Don't have to do it all in one day." She looked around the room. "Already I can see you've made some progress. Mr. Sullivan left this place in a shambles—the corral, the soddy, all of it."

"That's nice of you to say. We don't have much furniture, but I'm sure we'll get a few more pieces. I'd offer you some tea, but the fire went out."

"Not to worry. I brought you some hardtack." She reached into a pouch she had slung over her shoulder and pulled out a package wrapped in brown paper. "It's not much, but the good thing is it'll last forever."

I took the package and set it on the table. "Would you like a piece?"

"None for me. I'm sick of that stuff. But it serves its purpose on a long ride. Thought you might could use it before you get a kitchen set up."

"That was very kind." I opened the package and took out a rough-looking cracker. One bite told me that it would be best to have a glass of water handy to help it go down.

Ella looked me up and down and shook her head. "You're a right smart lady. You're probably used to better than this."

I gave a short laugh as I looked down at my dusty apron. "Not really. My life has been pretty chaotic since I arrived in America. But most of it's been better than where I came from."

"You one of them Irish? Lots of them in town."

"I am."

"You talk pretty good for an Irish gal."

"Thank you. I try."

"You're not here alone, are you?"

"No, Paddy went into town to get some supplies."

"He your husband?"

"No, more like a brother." I was tired of lying about Padraic. Plus, it no longer seemed worth the effort. What did she care what our relationship was? I didn't think she'd really mind.

"I see. You take care of yourself. I don't think they recognize common law around these parts."

I wasn't quite sure what she meant. "Oh?"

"You know, where if you stay with a feller for a certain length of time you're as good as married."

"Oh, no, it's not like that. We're here to find my brother. Then he'll join us, but Paddy and I, we're just friends, that's all."

"Sure," she said, nodding like she didn't believe a word. "I got one that's sorta like that. Only we're getting married if I have my say. Problem is I'm already hitched to someone else."

"Oh, where's your husband then?"

She shook her head as if she was trying to get away from something or someone. "Not sure. I heard he was back in town, but he comes and goes. Got tired of waiting around for him. Plus he wasn't so great when he was around. Just hope he doesn't try to get back in my life again. I let Bart move in with me a while back. He's got a bit of temper, too, but he's a good hand with the cattle. Hard to do all that on your own."

"You run cattle?"

"This land ain't much good for much else. Too alkaline to grow any real crops. Sagebrush likes it fine. Cattle's where the money is. I bought Sullivan's herd from him, such as it was, when he left. Mangy-looking bunch." She looked down at the floor as if deciding something, then up at me and said, "Also, I should just warn you, you lucked into a nice piece of land here. There's plenty of others who would have liked to have it. The cattle barons are out to grab anything they can get their hands on. Don't let them trick you into selling."

"Thanks for that information. I have heard they can be rather ruthless."

"You got that right."

There was a pause while we both looked at the ground. "I like your skirt," I finally said. "Is it split in two?"

"Yeah, a few of us women are starting to wear these split skirts so we can ride in the regular saddle. That sidesaddle business don't really work well when you're out all day on a horse."

"Yes, that makes sense. I've just been gathering up my skirt to ride, but I think I need to get a skirt like yours."

"You got any horses?"

"Not yet. I suppose we better do that."

"Only way to get around. Although those high-wheelers have started showing up in town."

"High-wheelers?"

"I guess they're called bicycles. Sit up high off the ground, big front wheel, smaller back wheel. You push on these pedals that go round and move the wheels. Funniest-looking things, but they can move pretty fast. However, you can take a mighty nasty fall if you come off one of them."

"I haven't seen one yet. How extraordinary."

"Yup. Couldn't get me on one of those things. I'm sticking with my horse." She pointed out the door. "He's called Spotty. Good little cow horse. He knows what he's doing." I looked out and saw her white-and-brown-spotted horse tied up near the corral, nibbling away at some tall grass. "He's a fine-looking animal."

Ella laughed. "Well, don't know if I'd go that far, but he's good at his job." She stood up and stretched. "I better keep moseying. Lots to do at my place. Come by anytime."

"Thank you. It's nice to know you aren't too far away."

Ella stopped in the doorway. "Brigid, it gets easier. I know it can seem hard at first. Pretty empty around here, but you'll find your way."

"Thank you again. I hope so."

"And get that fella of yours to make it legal. That would make you feel better in a hurry."

I couldn't help wondering if it would make me feel better—maybe that was what I needed, but why wasn't I more sure? I envied Ella. She seemed so certain of herself, so sure in this wild country. I admired that and was glad that she lived close by.

I stood in the doorway and watched her swing up on the saddle of her horse and ride off. A split skirt was what I needed. A horse would be good, too.

13

Later that day I heard horses hooves striking the dirt a ways out in the prairie. I hoped it would be Padraic but was wondering if it might be some Cheyenne Indians. They came around from time to time, Ella had said. I went and stood in the doorway, holding my hand over my eyes so I could see in the bright sun.

Two horses were headed this way, but only one had a rider. As they came nearer, I recognized Padraic by his hat. He was seated on the front horse and was leading the other horse by a rope. As they drew closer I recognized the other horse, too. It was the crazy filly that we saw at Bothwell's ranch, the one that no one seemed to be able to tame. The wild palomino mare. Padraic was bringing her here. I gasped. How could he have her?

I ran into the yard and they thundered in close to me. Padraic jumped off his dark horse and held both horses as I walked toward him.

"Come on slow," he said. "We don't need to spook her. She's been doing just fine coming along with us."

"Paddy, what have you done?"

He laughed and pushed back his hat. "We needed a horse, so I went over to Bothwell's place, thinking that way I could check on Seamus, too. I told him I needed a smart handy horse to get us around and to help with whatever cattle we might buy."

"Yes, but the other one?" I tried to hurry him along in his telling. "Why is she here?"

"Well, Bothwell remembered me. I asked about Seamus, and he said it's still going to be a while. When I settled on this horse, he told me that if I was interested he didn't want the palomino. He said if I thought you could handle her, I could take her along. He said that none of his men managed to calm her, not like you did."

"Oh, she's ours?"

"She's yours, Brigid." Padraic looked down at me. "She's your horse from now on."

For the second time that day I felt tears brim over in my eyes. I wept for the joy of it. My own horse. It was hard to take in that this was happening. I had hardly even dreamt of it. I looked at the golden filly and she nickered at me. Did she remember me?

"Oh, one more thing. She's been hurt. One of the cowboys who tried to break her whipped and kicked her. She's got wounds on her side that will need caring for, if you can get close to her."

"How could they do such a thing to her?" I asked. Padraic just shrugged.

I had a piece of that hardtack left in my apron pocket. I held it out to her, being careful to do it slowly and not make a move toward her. She must come to me, I knew this. She must decide that we could work together. She looked at my hand and snuffled. I spoke softly, "For you, my golden horse. Come and get it." I lifted my hand so it was at the height of her mouth.

She pawed the ground.

"Yup," I said, "it's all yours. Just as soon as you step over here." She put weight on the pawing foot and took one step forward. She was an arm's length from my hand. I resisted moving toward her, though it was hard not to give in to her brown eyes. She backed up a step and I stayed put. She looked at me and shook her head, her golden mane tossing down her neck.

"I know it's hard. But you can do it," I reassured her.

She took two steps and was within reach of my hand. Quickly she stretched forward and snatched the hardtack. Within a moment she backed up while chomping on the cracker.

"Good girl," I said. "It's just the beginning."

✳   ✳   ✳

Because the corral wasn't in good enough shape to secure the horses for the night, we tied the two horses close to each other. Then we weighted down their lead ropes with large rocks on the edge of the prairie where they would have plenty of grass to feed on.

I fetched a bucket of water and as I approached I could see the palomino watch me carefully, her ears tilting back. Not a good sign. I stopped until she brought her ears forward and then moved slowly until the bucket was in easy reach of both horses.

Standing only a couple arms' length from the filly, I could see the sun play off her golden coat like light off snow, and a name for her came to me: *Grian,* which means sunshine in Gaelic. Short and sweet, it fit her perfectly.

"Grian," I whispered.

She pricked up her ears, listening.

"You know your name, Grian. Soon we will be riding these prairies together, I'm sure of it."

14

O ur dinner that night was celebratory. We moved the table outside in front of the soddy and sat on two stumps that Padraic had found near the creek. I stuck a candle in an old bottle, and we lit it even though we were still in the gloaming. In this western land the sun set late in the evening, the light softening slowly in the sky.

I hadn't had time to get the beans going early enough for them to be ready to eat, but we had plenty of cheese and bread, and Padraic had thought to buy some apple butter that added a bit of sweetness to our repast. We both had a beer, and when we clinked our bottles together, I looked at him and asked, "So how are we doing?"

He laughed and held up his beer bottle in a salute to me. "I think we're doing grand. Look at us here, who would a' thought, king and queen of our own kingdom. What could be better?"

I knew he didn't expect me to answer that question, but I did. "It would be better if Seamus was here. Also, if we had more of a sense of what we're doing. Now that we have this land, whatever are we going to do with it?"

He reached out and squeezed my shoulder. "That's you, Brigid. Always with the planning and thinking ahead. Can't we just be here and enjoy what we have?"

"That's fine for a while, but pretty soon somebody better figure something out," I said, disappointed that he had made fun of my concerns.

"Like what?" he asked.

"Oh, I don't know. What are we going to do about the soddy? Are we going to run cattle? Do you know how to do that? Are we going to plant hay or whatever they grow here? Is it too late to do that? All I've ever planted was potatoes—but we know they can go rotten, and that's what got us here."

"I admit I don't know much about all that, but Seamus will surely know how to mind cattle," Paddy said, sounding pretty confident of this statement. I wished I felt the same.

"I would guess so. But what if he doesn't want to? Who knows if he'll even want to join us." I felt myself on the verge of tears again but drew them back with a big breath and said, "I just wish Seamus were here."

"Settle down, Brigid. He will be here soon enough. You're worrying about what might not even come to be. Let's take it slow. All will happen in its own good time."

"Maybe, but that isn't all I'm worrying about. I've actually been wondering what's going on between the two of us, you know."

He wrinkled his brow. "I thought you made that very clear last time we talked about it. As I recall, you said that you didn't want to make any decisions until Seamus was here."

"Yes, but I didn't know then that he would be out on the range for so long. I thought we'd find him as soon as we arrived. And here we are together all the time, and it's just concerning to me."

He leaned toward me. "How so?"

"I just don't know what to think. Do you know what you want?" I wasn't even sure where my uncertainty was coming from. "Do I even know what I want? And here I'm asking you."

"Listen, all is fine between us." He leaned in close to me and took my face in his hands. "We'll figure it out when the time comes. For me just this being together is enough for right now." At that moment I felt a weight lift off me. Maybe he was right about me worrying too much. I guess it came from being the oldest girl in my family. I wasn't that anymore. I was my own person.

Padraic was right: we could be fine at the moment. We had a place to live. We had two horses to ride. We had enough food to eat. We would have money as soon as Seamus came back, and I hoped that would not be long. The sky was clear and the weather was fine. So maybe we were fine too.

Paddy took my hand in his and said, "There is one thing I do worry about and that is that all this might be too hard on you. I'm not saying that you're not a good worker, but doing what needs to be done to start a ranch is not for everyone."

"How do you know what I can do? And what about you? You've never done ranching yourself. You're no cowboy, so who are you to talk?"

"You're right about that, but as a man I'm meant to live a bit tougher life than you. I want to make things easier for you. Just be sure that you let me know if you're having any misgivings."

"Aye, I will."

Padraic looked down at our joined hands and said, "I know you've had plans for bigger things than eking out a living on a claim, but we will have more money soon. And if we get this place going, then you can think about what you want, living in town, running a store. I know that would suit you better."

How did Padraic know this about me? I'd never really told anyone my plans—not even Seamus. I was afraid they'd laugh. But I had known for a while that I wanted to run a bookstore or a fine clothing store, even a shoe store. Something where my mind could be put to use and I would interact with other people, not just a bunch of mangy cattle.

One thing I knew for sure was that I never wanted to be a servant again, as I had been in New York and at the Hunts' in St. Paul. I learned so much working for the Hunt family—what it was like to move through a grand house, to be warm and safe, have wonderful food and a room filled with books. But it had also taught me to desire these grand things and to know I never wanted to be a domestic again.

"You're right," I told him.

"There's no right or wrong here. We just have to take it a step at a time. Even what's between us. No need to rush it." Then he leaned in and kissed me. A quick, simple kiss.

Just as quickly he pulled away. He stood up abruptly and put his hands on his hips, looking over at the horses. "One thing I know for sure, you're going to have your work cut out for you, taming that wild critter over there. And tomorrow I suggest we start mending that corral so we have a good place to keep those two fine horses. By the way, mine is named Smoky."

"That suits him. I just came up with the name for my horse—Grian."

"Oh, that suits her. She is like a beam of the sun. You've already got that far with her."

"Yes, and she knows her name. Watch." I shouted, "Grian!"

She turned her head and looked toward us.

"No fair." Padraic laughed. "Just because she heard you shout. That's why she looked."

"She already knows my voice. I told you my da was a horse whisperer, and I watched him careful as he trained the horses. I know that they must come to know your voice and to answer to it."

"I think she turned to see what you were shouting about."

"Believe what you want. I know that she's going to be my good horse very soon."

15

I was up before the sun, that excited was I to work with my horse, my Grian. Once in the night I had to peek out the door to make sure she was still there. Her golden coat shone in the moonlight. I stopped myself from going out to check on her. Let her have her peace, I thought. You need to take this slow. Remember what Da always said, "Haste is surely waste when it comes to a horse." And wouldn't Seamus be that surprised when he saw me riding on my own horse.

I threw on some clothes under the cover of my blanket. Not wanting to wake up Padraic, I crept outside to see how the two horses were doing. Both looking over toward the east, standing close together. I turned and watched as the sun just inched above the horizon and light swept across the land. It was a wondrous sight and I shivered in the coolness of the morning and the promise of it. As much as I wanted to walk over to check on the horses, I knew I better get a fire going and some breakfast in us before Padraic put us to work. Soon I had the coffeepot on the fire.

The horses snorted and stamped their feet. I looked up to see what they were on about and made out someone riding toward me. About a half-mile away, I couldn't see him that well, but he didn't look like a cowboy—there was no big hat on his head. Rather, he sported long black hair. I stared as he rode closer and came to see that the rider was an Indian. I assumed a Cheyenne. I stood up from where I'd been squatting by the fire and raised my hand in greeting.

He raised his hand too and rode closer to me, slowing his horse as he approached.

When he came within a rock's throw, I studied him. I had seen a few Indians in the town of Cheyenne and some too in Deadwood, but only at a distance. This one was closer to me than I had ever been before. He sat tall on his horse with only a blanket under him. His dark hair was parted in the middle and hung in two long plaits down his chest. He was wearing some kind of leather shirt that was fringed and then a leather wrap with pants on underneath that. Leather slippers were on his feet, which were gripping the sides of his horse.

He reined his horse in, and I saw that he used a cord wrapped around the animal's jaw but no bit.

"Hello," I said, not sure if he would understand me.

"Hello," he echoed back. He motioned toward the soddy, then said, "He here, Sullivan?"

"No, I'm sorry to say. He's gone. His wife died and he went back East."

"Back east." He pointed toward the east.

"Yes. Can I help you?"

He shook his head and his horse skittered around.

"Would you like some coffee?" I pointed at the coffeepot on the fire. It had come to a boil. I walked over and took it off the fire. I poured some in a tin cup. "Coffee?" I asked again.

"*Aho,*" he said and nodded his head.

I handed it up to him. Somehow I didn't think he was going to get off his horse, which was fine.

He took a sip and smiled. "Coffee, not bad."

"I try my best." I walked over and got a cup for myself.

"You here?" he asked.

"Yes, we came from Deadwood this past week."

"Oh, Deadwood," he pointed north.

"Yes, it's that way."

"We hunted here before," he said and circled the land with his hand. "But now no. We stay over there." He pointed to the west.

"Oh, you moved?"

"They moved us. Took the land."

I had heard about the drive to move the Cheyenne further west to provide land for the railroad and for the new arrivals. Which meant that I was living on what had been his land or his people's land. I didn't know what to say.

"Now buffalo gone too," he said in a somber voice.

"Yes, I've heard that most have been slaughtered."

"Hard to live without buffalo." He finished his coffee and handed the cup down to me.

"Are you hunting?"

"Sometimes. I come to see man who lived here before. He want some hides." He pointed to a pile of skins that were tied behind him on his horse.

I stepped forward and reached out to touch the skins, tawny red fur with white spots. "They're lovely. What animal?"

He thought for a moment, then said, "Antelope."

"Could I buy two from you?" I asked.

He nodded.

"Will you take money?"

He nodded again, then added, "*Aho.*"

"How much?" I had no idea what they might be worth.

"Fifty cents for the two," he told me.

I felt in the apron pocket that hung from my skirt and found two pieces of silver and handed them to him. He motioned for me to take two skins.

After untying the bundle, I just slid the two top hides off his pile. They would serve us well.

"Thank you for these," I said, holding one to my face to feel its fur on my cheek. "How do you say thank you?" I asked.

"*Neaese,*" he told me.

I tried to copy the way he had said it. "Nease."

"Thank you for coffee." He wheeled his horse around with a light touch of his hand on the rope and they rode off.

I stood watching him kick up a small dust whirlwind as they traveled away from me. The buffalo were gone and we were on his people's land. It reminded me of my last days in Ireland—the potatoes rotten in the ground, no land of our own. But now was I no better than the English?

❋   ❋   ❋

That entire day we spent repairing the corral. It felt good to be out in the sun, working with Padraic. He had to cut down a few small saplings by the creek and haul them back. While he was busy pounding in some of the uprights and resetting the crossbars, I stripped back the saplings and got them ready to be used in the fence. The good news was that most of the old wood could be reused. I wondered how long it had been since an animal had been kept in the enclosure.

I told him about the Cheyenne Indian and he looked somewhat alarmed. "Why didn't you wake me?"

"There was no need."

"You don't know that."

"I have come to trust my own feelings about men. It's a skill a woman needs in these parts. Just think of Deadwood, and you let me wander the streets alone there. I can take care of myself."

He looked down at the ground, then up at me, and said, "Yeah, but did you ever think that I might want to meet the Indian too?"

"Next time," I promised. We both laughed.

Every once in a while, I would gather a handful of tasty clover and bring it over to Grian. At first she would not move toward it until I set it down and stepped away. But soon she was coming toward me when I approached with my handful. Slow but sure.

The work of setting the corral to right was hot and sweaty. By the time we were done and the pen was secure, my blouse was drenched through. Padraic looked worse than I did, but at least he could take off his shirt.

"Let's move these horses into their new pen and go down to the creek to cool off," he suggested.

I walked slowly over to Grian and took hold of her rope as Padraic did the same to Smoky. With great pleasure and a good feeling of a job well done, we escorted them into the corral, removed their ropes, and fastened the gate behind us.

Padraic looked at me and said, "Race you," then took off running downhill toward the creek. I gathered up my skirt and hightailed it after him. But he had a head start and didn't have the disadvantage of an abundance of fabric to deal with.

"I let you win," I told him as I reached the bank of the creek just after him.

Padraic paid me no mind. He took off his boots and jumped into the water with just his trousers on.

I slipped off my skirt, kicked off my boots, and jumped in with only my bloomers and blouse on. The water felt wonderful, cold and bracing. Before I could sink into it, Padraic shot a handful my way. And we were on. Hooting and hollering, kicking and splashing and showering each other with water. Finally we sank down and sat at the bottom of the creek bed, up to our shoulders in the stream, and looked at each other and laughed till we were snorting.

"Your hair's come down. It's lovely like that," he said smiling at me.

"Well, your hair needs a cutting. You could almost tie it back now like a mountain man."

"Hey now, here I compliment you and you take off on me. That's neither fair nor kind."

I laid back on the water. "This feels delicious."

Padraic came up next to me and wrapped his wet arms around me. "This does feel rather delicious. May I have more?"

Without waiting for my answer, or maybe he saw the answer in my eyes, he leaned down and gently kissed my wet lips. I felt myself sliding away. It was all too much, the silkiness of the water, the gliding of our lips, the feel of his hot arms encircling me. I wanted it to go on forever. And indeed the kiss lasted a good long while until finally I managed to pull away from him.

"I couldn't help myself . . ." he started.

"No, 'tis fine. I mean I think we both needed it. It's been sitting between us for too long." As much as I wanted to throw myself back in his arms, I sat up and moved away. "I just think we need to watch ourselves until we know what we're going to do. There's a reason people wait until they're married."

He looked abashed. "Sure and you're right, of course."

16

Wouldn't you know as we walked across the long grass to our soddy, someone came riding up on a horse. And wouldn't you know that that someone was none other than Molly, my favorite waitress. Not a sight for sore eyes.

What led her to us? I wondered. Here was Padraic bare-chested with only a pair of pants hanging off his waist and me walking close to him, wet and sloshy. At least I had put my skirt back on so I wasn't so undressed. But we were definitely caught out.

"What have we here?" she asked, looking ever the lady in a crisp crinoline and broad-brimmed hat festooned with flowers. Her horse was a lovely sorrel with a handsome leather saddle and appeared very well behaved.

Padraic walked up and grabbed the head of the horse so she could dismount. "We just took a refreshing dip in our creek after working all morning on the old corral."

I said nothing. Let Paddy handle this one.

He held out his free hand and helped her dismount. I noticed she was riding sidesaddle, with a full skirt swishing around her. Obviously the new fashion of the split skirt wasn't for her yet. Why did she have to look so lovely when I was a sodden mess?

"You'll catch your death of cold," she laughed at him.

"Barely cooled me off. Nothing to fear." But at least he took her words to heart and slipped his shirt back on.

"What brings you out this way, Molly?" I asked in what I hoped was a friendly voice.

"Why, didn't Paddy tell you? He invited me to come out when I saw him in town. I'm sorry if this is an inconvenient time."

So Paddy had seen her when he had gone to town and had not thought to mention to me that she might stop by for a visit. I didn't dare look at him, sure that my anger would show. We certainly were not ready to entertain guests in our falling-down soddy. He should have known that.

"No, not at all." Padraic jumped in to assure her that all was well. "You're very welcome. Slipped my mind to let Brigid know. Won't you join us for dinner? It's not much but there's enough to share."

"Yes, I made a soup and you're more than welcome to share it with us," I added, trying to be gracious and glad that I had thought to put the soup on to simmer early that morning.

"How kind." She reached into her saddle bag and brought out a tin. "Well, I baked some biscuits this morning. With a nice knob of butter, which I also brought, they might be just the thing to have with your soup."

"How nice of you. That sounds like a feast. Excuse me while I change out of my wet clothes." I turned, happy to have a reason to go into the house and make myself presentable.

"Take your time. I'm sure Paddy can show me around." She walked over close to him and took his arm, not seeming to mind that he was still somewhat wet.

I brought the table back out into the shade of the soddy, much nicer sitting outside than in the damp of the house. Then I dragged out one trunk for Molly to sit on. Paddy and I could use the stumps like before.

I looked over and saw the two of them leaning on the top bar of the corral. Paddy was stretching out his arm, encompassing all of our land for her to be impressed by, and indeed she did look impressed. She looked like she was ready to swoon right into his arms.

A part of me wished that the rail would break and Miss Lovely would fall into a large pile of horse manure. And then another part of me was appalled that I could have such a thought. Why did that woman bring out the worst in me? Aside from the fact that she was making eyes at Paddy all the time and she looked so well turned out, I wouldn't mind having a woman friend. Especially one who wasn't afraid to ride out here on her own to visit. I promised myself that at dinner I would try to be more friendly, find out more about her, and see who she really was.

When the two of them came walking back from their stroll around the place, I had set the table with the little crockware we had and had found an old cup and put some early flowers in it.

"Well, I am a bit envious of you two. To have all this land and even a cozy little soddy until you can build something better. You've got a grand start on making a life for yourselves here. I'd love to be living out on the land like this, but town will have to do for me for a while yet."

"Don't you like your job? It seems like it's a good place to work," I asked, really wondering.

"It is that. I couldn't ask for a better boss. But it's not what I want forever." She gave me a quick, confidential look as if we felt the same way. "Brigid, you know what I mean."

I wasn't sure I did.

"This looks nice," Molly said. "It's like going on a picnic."

"That's a good way to look at it," I said.

"I'll just run down and bring back some beers for us all. I put them in the creek to cool," Paddy said, looking quite pleased with himself. He loped away and left the two of us sitting at that table.

"Your biscuits are so nicely raised. Might I have the recipe?" I asked, again trying to be more than civil to her. And truth be told, the biscuits did look rather perfect.

"Oh, I'll write it down for you. Are you able to read?" Molly asked with a tilt of her head.

Her question jarred me—what did she take me for? Shantytown Irish. "Yes, my mother taught me well," I told her, maybe a bit harshly.

"I didn't mean naught."

We sat uncomfortably for a moment, then she raised her eyes and said, "Your brother Paddy is an awfully nice man." Again, the word *brother* hit my ears, reminding me what Paddy had told everyone we were to each other.

"He's the spitting image of our da," I said, laying it on a bit thick. "But there's so many men in these parts and so few women. You must meet a lot of nice men."

"Oh, I meet them all right. But that's not to say I'd want anything more to do with them. A lot of the Irish came with the railroad, but they can be a rough crew. At least where I work caters to a better clientele."

"How'd you get out here then, Molly?"

"Well, I suppose like most everyone. Everyone said there were jobs galore in Cheyenne."

"Yes, it does seem a booming town."

"And now that we women have got the vote, it's even better. The first place that women have that right, and all because of a strong and insistent group of women. I'm one of them."

"I've heard about them, even up in Deadwood, but I'm not sure what all they do," I had to admit.

"They banded together—the swells, us working girls, and even the farm women—and demanded the right to vote. They're still working for more equality, owning property and the like. That's what you want, isn't it?"

"I hadn't given it much thought. I guess when you're working so hard to make enough money to live you can't always think about the bigger issues. You're lucky to work in town and all."

"Yes, but I am hoping to settle down sometime soon when I find the right man. I'm not getting any younger."

"How old are you, if you don't mind me asking?" I guessed she was older than I, but I wondered by how much.

"I'll be twenty-three this coming June. My ma was married when she was seventeen, but then she didn't have to fend for herself. And she'd known my da since they were wee ones."

"I'm just turning eighteen. I think my ma was about the same age when she met my da. But it took them a while to get married. They didn't have much themselves, not two pence to rub together," I explained.

"Well, I must tell you I've been thinking a lot about Paddy. That I have." She twirled a curl around her finger, then added, "He's one of the good ones, if you know what I mean." I knew exactly what she meant but decided to say nothing. She sounded like she might be looking for information on how to land him or even to get my blessing for going after him, but I was having none of that. Not after what I felt for him this afternoon, in the creek.

"And here he comes," I said, relieved we couldn't talk about him anymore.

* * *

The dinner went fine. Molly flirted with Paddy, asking his advice about everything under the sun, and I stayed busy, making sure everyone had enough to eat.

"What do you plan to do with your new homestead then, Paddy?" she asked him. "Are you thinking cattle or will you try to grow some hay?" I grew mad while thinking, It's mine too. I paid my share and I had more than a right to help make these decisions. But Padraic didn't seem to notice she had left me out of this conversation.

Finally Molly stood up and announced she had to get back to town.

"Do you want me to ride part the way back with you, Molly?" Padraic asked. "My horse needs the exercise. It will only take me a moment to get him saddled up."

"Well, then that would be lovely and ever so thoughtful of you." She turned to me and smiled her sweetest. "Brigid, you don't mind if I steal your darling brother for a bit, do you?"

I felt like screaming that Padraic wasn't my brother and that I did mind and anyways, why was she asking my permission? Instead I said, "I think that's a good idea. You never know who you might run into out in this vast prairie."

After they saddled up and left, I stayed seated at the table and watched as darkness crept over the land. I wondered how Paddy could be so fickle—one minute he's kissing me up and the next he's off escorting another woman home.

I looked at the moonless empty sky and felt quite alone, too.

17

The next morning I walked very nonchalantly into the corral where the two horses were standing, grazing. I tried to act as if I weren't even aware of them, not looking at them, not paying them any attention. When I got to the middle of the corral, I laid down on the ground and closed my eyes. For a few minutes, I stayed quite still, lying as calmly as I could, knowing full well the horses wouldn't do anything to hurt me. A horse will do just about anything to avoid stepping on someone unless they're scared or mad.

Finally I felt a soft nudge on my leg where my ankle was bared. I didn't move. Then something warm snuffled in my hair. I slivered open my eyes. Smoky was down by my feet, looking at me. And Grian was up by my head, bending over to stare into my face. I closed my eyes again and let them move around me.

After a while I slowly sat up. Smoky stayed where he was, but Grian skittered away. I had my eyes open, but I stayed so quiet, willing her to come to me. She walked around me and stood next to Smoky. When I saw she wasn't going to come any closer that day, I got up very slowly and left the corral.

The next day I brought one of the new hides with me into the corral and the pieces of Padraic's vest that I had cut out the night before. Standing on the far side of the corral, the two horses watched me. I sat down on the hide and started to sew. They both came closer. Smoky walked right up to me and stuck his nose in my work. I laughed, which made Grian shy away. But when I started petting Smoky's muzzle, Grian came close again. I could not quite touch her, but almost.

The next couple of days I spent a lot of time in the corral. I was in and out often. I fed them sweet grass, which Grian was starting to take from my hand. I groomed Smoky with an old brush, which he seemed to enjoy quite a bit. Grian watched as I stroked Smoky. As Grian got used to me being around, she followed me around the pen with Smoky by her side.

I just kept coming in and out of the corral many times a day, always feeding them both something. They had grazed the grass in the corral down to nubs. But that worked to my advantage. They were always glad to see me with some new goodies. Grian stopped skipping away when I opened the corral door. Instead she would watch me for a second and then come toward me. I hadn't tried to reach out to her or pet her. I figured it was best at first to let her make most of the overtures.

❉ ❉ ❉

One day, sewing on Paddy's vest, a wave of dreariness came over me. With all my heart I wished my father could come to help me with my horse. I remembered him telling me how with one very obstinate and unruly horse he ended up rocking the animal back and forth and then tipping it and throwing it down on the ground. I had no intention of doing that to Grian, but a wave of homesickness for my dear father and my whole family swept over me. I missed my family so much. I missed being around other people. I missed the bustle of a town. It was different for Padraic. He seemed happy enough, fixing up the soddy, making some furniture for us, riding into town to get supplies. But I felt stuck out in the middle of the vast plains—empty and desolate. I was not used to being so alone; never in my whole life had I been without the bustle of people around me.

As these thoughts came over me, I set down my sewing, put my face in my hands, and started to weep. The tears were like a slow seep of spring water, just running down my face. I made very little noise, trying not to let it build into sobs. Then I felt something nudge my head. When I looked up there was Grian with her muzzle right in my hands. I tentatively rubbed her nose and she didn't move away. She had come to comfort me, and it just about broke my heart.

She nickered at me. The sound was so sweet that I started to laugh. At that she raised her head high and gave an answering whinny.

"Oh, Grian," I said.

For the next step I needed Padraic's help. I asked him to saddle up Smoky while I put a loose rope around Grian's neck. He opened the corral gate and climbed up on Smoky. I followed, leading Grian out of the corral for the first time. Smoky walked slowly ahead with Padraic riding him and I was behind, leading Grian with the lightest tension on the rope. We made a big loop in the yard, just walking at a steady pace. Grian moved easily at my side.

When we put them back in the corral, Padraic was as excited as I was. "Grian is really coming along. You have the gift of your father, you do. A horse whisperer in the making."

The following day, for the first time I was on top of Grian, but not riding her, rather draped over her back with the blanket under me. I hung loose like a sack of potatoes—my legs on one side of her and my arms and head on the other—and let her wander around the corral. She would stop every once in a while and look back at me, but surprisingly she didn't seem very bothered. It wasn't the most comfortable position for me, so I didn't stay that way for too long, but I was thrilled that she had been so easy about the extra weight. However, as Padraic pointed out, "You don't weigh that much. Maybe she didn't even notice you were there."

Everything I did with her, I did slow and easy, talking to her the whole time, whispering the way my father had taught me. He used to say that it didn't really matter what you said, just that you said it with love. That's what the horses needed to hear. Never be angry, but always be kind.

It was a good way to live.

18

"I'm going for a walk," I told Padraic. "I wish I could ride Grian but she's not quite ready."

He looked up from the chair he was constructing out of an old crate and a couple of pieces of lumber. "Fine day for it. Where to?"

"I think I'll go over the rise and visit Ella."

"Ella?"

"You know. I told you that this woman came to visit while you were gone. It was near to a week ago. About time I returned the favor. I wish there was something I could bring her, but we've so little ourselves. I haven't started baking—but I'll try soon with that cast-iron pot."

"I'm sure that your sweet company would be enough for anyone, especially out here in the country."

"I'm just letting you know in case you missed me."

"Kind of you," he smiled at me.

The two of us were in a good spot with each other—warm toward each other but careful not to overdo it, worried one of us might take it the wrong way. It was almost as if we had skipped the courting part and gone straight through to being an old married couple. I had to think it was comfortable, until I remembered the kiss in the creek, the rush of it, the wanting more.

I set off in what I was sure was the right direction. After all I had watched Ella as she got on her horse and rode off. The only thing was I didn't know how far away her place was.

I was curious about the strange plants that grew out of this dry red soil. There were all different kinds of cactus, some bigger than men, and some the size and shape of a pin cushion. One thing they all had in common was prickers. I would be careful to guide Grian away from them if they were in our path. At the top of one tall cactus I even saw a bird perched on a nest. It was all brown and thrust out its chest to sing a tuneful song. I slowed down to listen to the lovely sound.

As I walked to the top of the rise and looked down over the land I could see a building off in the distance, sitting out in the land like a wooden box. That must be her house, as I could see no other. I figured that it would have taken me about a half an hour to walk there and I wasn't far wrong.

The sun was warm on my back and I wished I hadn't worn my shawl. I took it off my shoulders and wrapped it around my waist. I breathed in deep. It felt good to be out in the world, not cooped up in our cramped soddy, trying to make the best of the small space. Out on the plains, the sky was enormous, reaching to all the ends of the earth. To look up at the blue was to fall into it forever.

"What's a pretty thing like you doing out here?" a voice came from behind me.

When I turned I saw a rangy man slouched on a pinto. He had come up behind so quiet I hadn't even heard a sound. That alone was scary, and then the way he was looking at me didn't make me feel any better.

"Heading to a friend's house, right over there." I pointed to show him I wasn't lost and didn't need his help.

"You coming from that place back yonder?"

I saw no reason to evade his question. "Yes, we're homesteading it."

"Sure you are. Snatched it right under the nose of my boss man."

This surprised me. I had no idea anyone else was interested in our land. "Is that so?"

"He's not very happy about that."

"Who might he be?" I asked.

"The biggest sugar himself. Mr. Bothwell. He's been wanting that land for some time. It adjoins his at the far end, and it's on the creek. Not happy at all." His horse jostled him and he pulled it in tight.

"Sorry to hear that, but we heard about it and went to the land office right away."

"Any chance you'd sell up?" he asked.

"Not at the moment," I said.

"I'll let the boss know." Without another word, he turned his horse so quickly that it reared and then took off the other way. I was glad to see the back of him.

When I arrived within hailing distance of Ella's house, I heard voices. But then I remembered that Ella had said she lived with a man. Maybe we could have the two of them over. I was sure Padraic could use the company too.

As I walked a bit closer, I could tell there were two people talking, or rather yelling, and they sounded very angry at each other. I stopped in my tracks. What was I walking into? Another few steps and I could make out the words that were being thrown back and forth. Even though I knew I was eavesdropping, what could I do in such a situation but listen?

"I seen you with that swaggering hooligan. I knowed who he is," a man's voice crowed.

"So what?" I recognized Ella's voice, but she sounded meaner than I could have imagined her. "You got a problem with that?"

"So what? I'm living here with you. I got my rights."

"I didn't ask you to move in with me. You just did."

"You did so, and you said if I worked hard this place would be half mine." The man's voice came back at her.

"Yeah, maybe I did, but you haven't worked hard enough and certainly not long enough."

"Oh, you think you're so smart. You think you can make something out of this place. Well, you're as wrong as wrong can be. This homestead is too small to do anything with. You can't run cattle and you can't grow nothing."

"As if you know anything about it."

"More than you."

I stayed stock still. I wasn't sure if I should announce myself or quietly turn around and walk back home. But then I heard a noise I couldn't ignore. Something hard hitting on flesh and an outraged scream. I couldn't pretend I wasn't there and didn't know what was happening in the house. I couldn't walk away if Ella was being hurt.

I rushed to the door and flung it open. What I saw was not what I thought I would see. A man was lying prostrate on the floor with his arms over his head, trying to protect himself while Ella held a large wooden spoon and was going after him with it, hitting him whenever she had a chance.

"Hallo . . . ?" I said.

They both stopped in midfight and turned and looked at me.

"I just came by," I managed to say.

Ella lowered the spoon but still gave the man a kick as she walked toward me. "This here chickenshit was trying to tell me my business. He got no right to do that. I own this place—lock, stock, and barrel. I filed for it and I want to keep it. He's got other thoughts that aren't going to happen. Talking about selling out from under me. No way in hell."

Taking advantage of my entrance, the man scrambled to his feet and hightailed it out of the house, pushing me out of the way as he passed by. From the little I had seen of him, he appeared a scrawny thing, not much bigger than Ella. He sported a moustache and had thin, squinty eyes. He reminded me of a weasel as he slunk away.

"I was worried he was hitting you," I said.

"He couldn't hit the broad side of a barn." She sat down in a chair by the table and pushed one out for me. "Just a stupid ninny. I don't know why I ever joined up with that yack. Stupidest thing I ever done."

"What were you fighting about?" I asked, sitting down across from her. Her face was red and sweaty, and her hair was coming out of her bun.

"Nothing you need to be concerned about. He's just sticking his nose in where it shouldn't be. I worked hard to get this place. He thinks we should sell, but it's not going to happen. He just wants the money."

"He said he saw you with someone?" I asked, since Ella didn't seem to mind talking about what had happened.

"Oh, that's nothing. My good-for-nothing husband showed up in town, and I happened to run into him. We just had a little talk, not too cozy. If he thinks I'm going to pay him the money he claims I owe him, he's got another think coming. He left me high and dry without a word. He can't come creeping back into my life, that's one thing I know for sure."

"Hope he doesn't cause you any trouble. Either of them."

"Oh, I'm not scared of those two. They came out of the same barrel, losers. What's the matter with me that I keep choosing the wrong fellas? I let them honeyfuggle me, and then I don't know how to get rid of them."

I looked around her house. It was quite a bit nicer than our soddy.

First of all, it was built of wood, not sod, which made it stay cleaner, and second, it had three glass windows, which let in a lot more light. A potbelly stove had the place of honor in the center of the room with a rocking chair set right in front of it. In the far corner was the carved wooden bedstead big enough for two people to sleep in comfort.

"You have a such a nice place," I said. "The house looks real sturdy, and you've made it so comfortable."

"Well, it's taken me a couple years to get it like this, but I'm happy with it. You should have seen the tent I lived in for the first year. Pretty rough. Just about froze my ass off. I think that your soddy will be warm enough if you can get a little stove in there."

"Yes, that'd be good for heat, and I'm going to need something for cooking when it gets colder. I like the looks of the one you have."

Ella was silent for a moment, then wrung her hands together. "Sorry you had to walk in on that. Bart isn't such a bad guy. He just makes me so mad sometimes and then I fly off the handle. He's always trying to tell me what to do. I wish he would just let me do this all my own way."

"I understand. It's hard out here, and you become so dependent on the other person."

"I bet you never get angry the way I just did. You seem like you're pretty level-headed."

I thought about it for a moment. "I don't get mad too often, but when I do I can be a bear."

Ella laughed. "I'd like to see that. You ever get mad at your spark?"

"My what?"

"Your sweetie, your beau."

I had to think about it. Padraic wasn't perfect, but he was pretty easy to be with. "Not really. Not yet anyways. He's a good fella."

She leaned back in her chair so far that I was afraid she was going to pitch over backwards. "What's really going on with you and this fella? If he's as nice as you say he is, I don't get why you don't snare him."

"It just feels too soon for me. I like him fine. In fact, I think I love him, but I don't feel like I know my own mind yet. This is all so new to me, and I want to be sure about what I'm doing. I'd hate to get stuck where I don't want to be." My thoughts went to poor Mrs. Sullivan, having a baby in that soddy and not living long enough to hear it cry. That was not the future I had planned for myself.

"You're young," Ella said. "How old are you, anyways?"

"Turned eighteen a few months ago."

"Not even twenty yet. You might be right to wait. I married my first husband when I was twenty-one, and that turned out to be a mistake. I'm thirty now and I still don't know how to pick a good man."

"You think Bart's gone for good?" I asked.

"Nah. He'll be back. He always comes back. I think he likes the way I treat him, which is the saddest thing of all." I didn't know what to say to that. "I'd like it better if he'd fight back once in a while, show me he's a real man."

Again I felt like I was in over my head. Not that people didn't squabble back home, but it seemed like all human interactions out here in the west were more dramatic, more violent. Even me, shooting a man in the leg.

19

Every day Grian grew easier with me. When I opened the gate to the corral, she would not move away from me anymore. I could now rub her muzzle between her eyes and tell that she liked it. I could touch her anywhere and she would move in or out of my hands. Trust was there in her eyes.

Now she watched me. When I moved around her, she followed me with her eyes with her head held upright and her ears pricked forward. She seemed to like me to be there with her. I could tell she was less afraid of me. We were both working toward that goal.

The halter I had made out of rope was now on her all the time. She didn't flinch when I put the blanket on her. I had even put the saddle on her and walked her around so she could get used to the feel of it.

She was ready. Was I?

Then the day came. I couldn't wait any longer. I knew it was time. That morning I dressed in my new split skirt for the first time. I had splurged and bought it in town. I could always copy a pattern from it and make myself another one, but I wanted the first one to be store-bought. A treat for me.

I knew that this first attempt to ride her might be rather decisive. My father had told me, "Let them know you're in charge, but let them know you're a team. Work with them, not agin 'em."

When I walked into the corral, Grian looked up from her grazing and then walked toward me. What a good sign, I thought.

As I attached two lead ropes to her halter, she blew out her nose at me, which made me laugh. The lead ropes I would use as reins to guide her, but I would also use my whole body as my father had taught me. "You shouldn't need to use the reins if you're clear which way you want them to go," he always said. Now I wished I had listened more carefully to all he had tried to teach me.

The blanket went on easily. She had no trouble standing still for me anymore. I slowly put the saddle over it and reached under her belly to fasten the girth. Grian danced a bit, but I was holding the ropes and was able to settle her down quickly. She was all set.

I led her around the corral and let her get used to the saddle, showing her she had nothing to fear. Smoky watched us but then went back to grazing. His presence did seem to calm her.

After a turn in the ring, I gathered the ropes over her neck, put my foot in the stirrup, and swung up into the saddle. Grian took a couple of steps backwards and shook herself like she was trying to get rid of a fly, but then she stood stock still as if she couldn't possibly move, as if she were really taking in what was happening to her, deciding if she would allow it.

Leaning over her neck, I slowly rubbed her down while whispering sweet things in her ear. She stamped her feet but did nothing more than that. I could have crowed with delight. There I was, on top of my own horse for the very first time, feeling on top of the world.

Unfortunately, Padraic chose that moment to walk around the corner of the house and saw me sitting on Grian. He took his hat off and threw it in the air, yelling "Yahoo!"

And that did it.

Grian skipped, then gave a slight buck. I was thrown sideways in the saddle and my hands flew up, yanking back on the reins. Jerking the reins made Grian buck again, only much more violently this second time. I got thrown way up on her neck and I could get no good grip. I could feel myself slipping. I thought of trying to right myself by pulling the reins tighter, but I knew that wouldn't work. It would only make Grian more nervous and scared and cause her to buck again. She was already dancing up a storm. So I decided to just let go.

I kicked my feet loose from the stirrups, let the reins fall away, and slipped out of the saddle, falling to the ground. Grian danced away, then stopped and came back to me. I had landed on my side but rolled over on my back to check that I was okay. Grian stuck her muzzle in my hair and sniffed.

"Hey, there," I said, while rubbing her nose.

I wasn't hurt, except my pride. For one thing, Padraic had seen the whole incident. My hat falling off, my new skirt up over my knees, and I lay sprawled in the dust of the corral. Padraic walked over and leaned on the top bar of the corral, looking down at me. "You were in the saddle for a moment. You need any help?"

"I'm fine. It is all your fault, you know. What were you thinking, yelling like that? You know better." I rolled onto my side, not quite ready to get up. "I wish you would just go away and leave me to it."

"I thought you had her under control."

"She's ten times the size of me and barely trusts me. If I have control, it's only because she gives it to me."

He opened the gate, sauntered over, and helped me to my feet. "You've got to get on her again, you know." He was right, of course. I knew what I had to do, even though much of me wanted to go sit in the soddy and have a cup of tea and lick my invisible wounds.

"I know and I will. But I'm asking you to please leave the corral. You're no help at all," I said sharply to Padraic.

"I could hold the horse and give you a hand up into the saddle," he suggested.

"No, I don't need you to do that. And you won't always be around. I have to be able to do this on my own." I brushed myself off. He turned around and let himself out the gate, but then stood and watched me clamber up on my horse.

"Please go away, Padraic," I told him. "You know you're not helping matters at all, at all." I watched him as he went to the front of the soddy and sat down on one of the stumps. I didn't care if he watched, just so he didn't interfere and stayed quiet.

Grian was patiently standing by. I rubbed her nose and ran my hand down her neck. "You're a good one, my lovely golden horse. You did nothing wrong. That was a loud noise that made you jump. I don't blame you."

In one hand I gathered the reins together at the bottom of her mane. With the other I grabbed hold of the saddle and steadied myself as I put my boot in the stirrup. Pushing off with the other foot I swung up into the saddle. Grian stood for it all. I patted her on her neck and told her how well behaved she was. Then I clicked my tongue and urged her forward, giving her a snap on the rump with the end of the reins.

Grian craned her neck around and looked back at me as if to say, "Whatever was that for?" I tapped her on the rump again and she took a step. Leaning forward with the movement of her body, I clucked my tongue and she stepped right out into a fast walk. I eased her around the ring of the corral, past Smoky, who gave us a look and went back to grazing.

Leaning forward in the saddle I urged her on. After taking two long strides she broke into a trot and I tried to get into her rhythm. The corral was too small to try to gallop her—that would have to wait until I took her out. But after circling the ring a few times at a trot, I pulled her in and she slowed down to an easy, gentle walk.

Once more around the ring and then I tried turning her around by gently pulling her head in the direction I wanted her to turn and by using my body to show her the way. She turned and continued in the opposite direction as smoothly as I could have ever wished. When I reined her in, she came to an immediate stop. No bucking this time. I could feel the tenseness easing out of her flanks. She became still.

For a few blessed moments, I stayed in the saddle, savoring what we had done together. I could tell that she had been able to sense what I wanted her to do if I was clear with my directions. Soon I would be able to take her out of the corral, but we had done enough for today. I was happy with how my filly was coming along.

Riding her I could feel how tightly wound she was, but that wasn't all bad. Grian had lots of spring in her step and lots of energy to let loose. The good news was I knew she hadn't been ruined by the bad treatment she had received at the Bothwell ranch. I was so glad that it hadn't gone on for too long before she was given to me. Spirited she was, and it would have been a shame if that spirit had been beaten out of her.

Grian just needed to know she could trust the person who was on her back. I swore I would try to live up to that trust. More than anything, I wished my father could see me riding on top of my own horse, one that I had tamed to the saddle. He would have been so proud.

Part III

The Hanging

I have been thinking to-day,
As my thoughts began to stray,
Of your memory to me worth more than gold.
As you ride across the plain,
'Mid the sunshine and rain,—
You will be rounded up in glory bye and bye.

—Cowboy Songs

20

The day had come when I knew it was time to take Grian off for a ride through the plains on my own. I had ridden her around our homestead, and she was getting easier and easier to handle, as if we were growing and moving together. Once a rabbit jumped out at her feet and she barely balked. I too was feeling much more secure in my seat again. I hadn't ridden that much since coming to America.

First I thought to swing by Ella's and see how she was doing. I had been meaning to check up on her and hoped she was doing well. I couldn't get out of my mind the argument I had overheard and hoped that her fella had either settled down or left. The words I had heard were not kind ones.

And I wanted to show off my horse.

＊　＊　＊

When I entered the corral, she came right over to me, sniffing me and looking to see if I had brought any goodie for her. She liked carrots, and every once in a while I'd bring her one.

I saddled her up and sprang to her back without a care in the world. The weather was perfect, the soddy was starting to feel like home, and Padraic and I were getting along just fine. I had started to see a way forward for myself. Sure and I didn't want to live in the soddy forever, but for the time being it suited me just fine. Once we were all set up on the place, I could try to find a job in town, something that would be more enjoyable for me since I couldn't see myself happy as a rancher's helpmeet.

And it kept getting closer to the day when Seamus would get back from his work on the trail. Padraic had checked in at Bothwell's, and the rancher had said it could be any day now. I could hardly wait, so anxious was I to set my eyes on my dear brother again.

❋ ❋ ❋

Ella's homestead looked deserted when I rode up. The door stood open and so I took a look inside. The room was tidy. Nothing seemed amiss. She must have gone off into town. Maybe her partner had taken himself off too. I'd come back another day.

Not wanting to return home so soon, I decided to ride out west of her place. The land stretched flat all around me. Such an odd feeling being able to see the horizon on all sides. It made me feel both vulnerable and very alive, as if all were open to me. I wanted to believe that.

A ways in front of me I spied what looked to be an oasis, a couple of large cottonwood trees, which usually meant that a source of water was nearby. I headed over that way to take a look and to give Grian a drink.

❋ ❋ ❋

All my happiness flew away when I rode down to the oasis and looked up into the branches of the cottonwood tree. A flutter of white had caught my eye, but as I looked closer I saw what was hanging in the tree.

A body swayed in the wind. A woman hanging dead—and I knew her.

I jumped off Grian and ran to the swaying body. Ella's feet were just above the ground. When I reached up and grabbed her hand, it hung loose and empty, the life having flown out of it. Somehow I had to get her down. I couldn't stand the thought of leaving her hanging like that. It wasn't right and it felt horrible. Surely a desecration.

Whoever had done this horrible thing must have flung the rope over a branch, but then they tied it, at about shoulder height, to the trunk of the tree. I forced myself to go over there and worked at untying it. The weight of Ella's body kept the rope so taut that I had a hard time making any headway on the knot, but finally it began to loosen. With a snap it came undone and Ella's body fell to the ground. I ran to her and bent over her crumpled form, no life left in it.

By this time I was beside myself. Tears were streaming down my face, but I tried not to make a sound. I was shaking and sobbing, but I didn't want to give in to my crying and spook Grian. I pulled myself together, wiping my face with my sleeve. I couldn't leave her this way. I knelt down by Ella's limp form. Her face was toward the ground, and I was glad I didn't have to look into it as I tried to figure out what to do next with her body.

Though I didn't know if she was of the Catholic faith, for myself I needed to say a prayer over her as I knelt there. I made myself touch her shoulder, as the priests always did, and then I intoned:

Holy death,
hopeful death,
shining death,
comforting death,
forgiving death.

Death without anguish,
death without shadow,
death without dying,
death without fear,
death without sorrow.

After I said the prayer, I hoped with all my heart that she had found peace, and that she would be welcomed as she arrived in heaven.

Then I stood, knowing I had more to do. I couldn't get her on my horse, I was sure of that. Grian was too new to handle the extra weight of such a load. And after all my hard work, there was no way I would scare my horse again. I came to see that I'd have to leave Ella there, under the cottonwood trees, and ride to get some help. I thought of going back to her house to see if Bart had returned, but then I recognized that might be a very bad idea.

With a start I saw that this killing could be Bart's handiwork. He hadn't been at the homestead, so maybe he was gone. Maybe he had done this and left her hanging in the wind. It became clear that I needed to ride back home and find Padraic, then one of us could go into town for the sheriff.

"What happened to you?" I asked Ella.

But she lay as still as a stone.

Her bound hands were bloodied as if she'd been pounding someone hard with them. As if she'd been fighting for her life—which she had. I could almost picture the struggle in my mind's eye. Her kicking and screaming and hitting out as hard as she could. No use it was.

I hated to leave her like that, facedown in the dirt. I gently turned her over and arranged her more comfortably, so she looked as if she might be sleeping. Hard it was to look at her face, the eyes rolled back and her jaw slack. Her hair had come down and was wrapped around her neck, probably had been caught in the rope. Little as I wanted to do it, I forced myself to examine her, to try to understand what had happened to her. I had to wonder if the man who had done this carried some marks on his face, maybe a way to identify him.

I took off my shawl and covered her with it, pulling it up and over her face. That was all the protection I could offer her at this moment. And to be true, she needed no more.

It came to me that I knew so little about Ella. I didn't know if she had any family around abouts. There was Bart, and then she had mentioned that her husband had been seen in town. I trusted neither of them.

As I turned away, I said another prayer that whoever did this would be found and brought to justice. I swore I would do what I could to make sure that happened.

21

ensing my urgency, Grian stretched out her legs and we flew back over the land—both to get away from what we had left and to reach the safety of our own homestead. Happy was I to see the soddy top the horizon.

Padraic looked up, startled, as we galloped into the yard. He smiled at me, then frowned when he saw my face. "What is it, my Brigid?" he asked, grabbing the reins and pulling Grian to a full stop.

"Worse than ever." I slid off my horse and fell into his arms. "I found her, there was nothing I could do," I gasped.

"Whoa." He grabbed my shoulders and held me apart from himself. "What're you trying to tell me?"

"She was hanging as dead as can be."

"Who and where?"

"Ella. I found her hanging from a tree. No one was around, but someone did this to her as her hands were bloodied and tied behind her back."

"No, how can that be?"

"I think she must have been murdered. Whatever, she's dead." As I said these awful words, I felt a tearing in myself. As I said them out loud, I came to know them more deeply.

"And you found her so?"

"I did. But I got her down and covered her. Who could do such a despicable thing?"

"I can't imagine it. Terrible this thing is."

"Padraic, we must do something to find out how this all happened and to punish the man responsible. It could be her partner and he might be trying to get away." I was near frantic with the thought of her left out there

101

alone. What if an animal found her? What if whoever did this to her came to take her away and bury her?

"Brigid, this is not for you to take on. Whatever has happened it is a job for the sheriff." He let go of me as if to ready himself for his ride, but I didn't want him to leave me.

I grabbed him back. "Since I found her, don't you think I should go with you and be the one to tell the story of it all?"

Padraic was about to say no, he was shaking his head, but then he looked up at me and his eyes softened. "I guess you should. I don't want to leave you here, but are you up for another ride?"

❊   ❊   ❊

The ride into town did seem a long one. I was glad to see the first buildings appear down the road from us and a wagon pass by filled with supplies. We were approaching civilization, such as it was in the west.

We stopped a man on horseback and asked where we might find the sheriff. He told Padraic the way but added, "If he's there. But he comes and goes." Laramie County was still such a new establishment that the position of sheriff might not even be a full-time job. I prayed that he'd be in his office so we could get this all taken care of as soon as possible. Thoughts of Ella laid out on the plains made me so sad and angry.

We found our way to the office and knew we were there by the sign hanging over the door: LARAMIE COUNTY SHERIFF. After tying the horses to the rail, I swiped a hand down my skirt as if that would make me more presentable, might remove the dust at least, then followed Padraic into the office.

There was not much to see: a desk, a chair, and a white-haired man with a long moustache bent over some papers. Behind him was a framed map of a geographic survey of the United States.

"Sir, are you Sheriff Sharples?" Padraic asked when the man didn't look up as we approached.

That caused him to lift his head and he squinted at us. "Yup, that's what they tell me. What can I do you for?"

We introduced ourselves and the sheriff motioned us to take the two seats placed in front of his desk. I took a good look at him and decided when he sat up tall he did look like a sheriff with his gold badge and all. His moustache was so wide it almost touched his ears, but the really odd thing about it was it had white ends and was darker in the middle. I tried not to stare.

When I couldn't find the words, Padraic broke the silence. "It's about our neighbor, Ella Bates. Brigid found her dead. She'd been hanged." Padraic then told him, "We live out by the Sweetwater."

"A woman?" He sounded as if he didn't believe us. "She's been hanged, you say? How so?"

"Yes, I found her," I said, when the sheriff didn't seem to be fully understanding the matter. "She had been strung up with a heavy rope and was hanging from a tree. She was dead. Somebody killed her."

"You sure she didn't do it to herself?" he asked. "Some women just can't handle the lonesomeness out there."

"From what I could see that would have been impossible," I told him. "She was too high up and her hands were bound behind her back. Plus, I had talked to her only the day before and she seemed of sound mind to me."

"What'd you say her name was again?" he asked.

I was getting very impatient with him. From his tone of voice I could tell he wasn't quite taking this all in. "Her name was Ella Bates and she lived just a ways from us, the other side of the creek. I think she's been in Cheyenne for a while."

"Ella Bates. That's ringing a bell with me. I think I'd heard some talk that she'd been picking up calves that didn't belong to her out on the range. That can make folks mighty angry."

"How could she take someone else's cattle as her own? Aren't they all branded?" Padraic asked.

"Not the yearlings. Lots of them haven't been branded yet."

"But to kill her? Who knows, she might have done it by mistake. Maybe she thought they were hers," I suggested. "That's not the way to handle such a minor offense."

"Out here it's not minor. Cattle rustling is a dangerous game." The sheriff sucked his lower lip, then said, "Sometimes that's the only way to handle it. Yup, they call it 'wearing the hemp necktie,' although I suppose in her case it might be a necklace." He gave a slight chuckle.

"I do not find this funny." I stood up and leaned on his desk so he could see how serious I was. "What're you going to do?"

"My job." He took a swipe at his large moustache. He gave me a stare back and was no longer smiling. I could tell I wasn't helping matters by goading him. "Since you weren't a witness to this event, you can't be of much help. I'll try to find out what happened, but I'm still thinking she might have done it to herself. Women get awful lonesome out on the plains. It wouldn't be the first time." He shrugged.

"Her hands were bloodied like she'd been fighting someone off. When you see her, I think you'll change your mind and want to find out who did this to her," I told him straight out.

"If you're so sure about someone doing this to her, do you have any ideas as to who it could be?" he asked me.

I looked over at Padraic, but he just shrugged too. "Well, I do, as a matter of fact," I told him. "I can name two men who had something against Ella. She had a partner out there on her ranch, Bart, and they had had words recently. That I do know because I was there and I witnessed it. Plus, she said that her ex-husband has been seen around town, asking about her. Not sure what his first name is. There's two good leads for you."

"Thank you kindly for your help. If what you're saying is true, this must be looked into. I'll send a man with a buckboard out to fetch her. One of the churches will likely claim her."

I explained to him where she was—the big cottonwood was a good marker for them to look for after they went to her house.

Finally Padraic spoke up. "Sheriff, if we can be of any more help, please let us know. This has been awful distressing for Brigid, and we would like to know that justice is being done."

The sheriff shook his head, his white hair falling over his brow. "Justice takes many forms out here. For all I know, she might already have received all the justice she deserved."

I could not stand this lawman's opinion about such a death. "No one deserves what Ella got—to be hanged like that. I will check back in with you to see how you're coming along on this case."

"I'm sorry that you had to be the one to find this young woman, Miss Reardon. It's not a pleasant sight, but does happen from time to time.

Try to calm yourself. And please let me know if you think of anything else that might pertain."

With that we took our leave. As soon as we stepped outside his office, I turned to Padraic and said, "I don't think he will do much to find out who did this to Ella. But I will not let it go. I don't care what she's done, she didn't deserve to be killed."

"Brigid, can you let it be?"

I could hear the pleading in his voice and I knew it came only from concern for my well-being. But I also knew what to say to make him understand why I needed to pursue this incident, and so I said it: "What if it were me, Padraic? Could you leave it be?"

22

Padraic and I had a quiet dinner that night. He didn't say much and I figured it was because he didn't know what to say. I didn't say much because I was wrung out and had no words left.

To do the dishes I went to fetch a bucket of water from the creek. It was more than my turn, not that Paddy would ever say that to me. I had to be mighty quick to grab the bucket before him. We had been living in the soddy for nearly two weeks now, and we were settling into a routine of duties.

When I got to the creek, I sat down on a rock and watched the water flow. I wondered where it was going, where it would end up. I threw a leaf into the stream and watched it jitter and jump along as it was carried away from me. Would it make its way out to the ocean or get caught on a branch?

The bigger question was where would I end up. Ella's death had pulled the heart out of me. Look how hard she had tried to make something of her life, how she was going to raise cattle and grow her ranch. I didn't think I had her energy or desire for that life the way she had. How would I manage when even she couldn't make it?

If Mr. Bothwell wanted our place, maybe we could sell it to him and recoup our money plus a bit extra. But I knew that Padraic was set on making a go of it as a ranch. Waiting for Seamus to show up was getting harder every day.

My little leaf hit a rock and capsized. Made me give a hiccup of a laugh. Sometimes things happened, no matter how hard you tried to be okay. I could hear my father telling me, "Success consists of getting back up one more time than you fall." I was tired of falling but knew I had to get up again. We had been at the soddy for a little over a month, and I was surprised by how much work it was every day.

I dragged myself up, filled my bucket with water, and started back to the soddy. There were chores to do before sleep. I had finished sewing the vest for Padraic and wanted to give it to him this night. Such a gift might make both of us feel better after the hard day we had had, me for the giving and he for the getting.

*　*　*

"I've never had such a fine vest as this," Padraic declared when he slipped it on over his rather soiled shirt. "To think that you made this yourself."

"With my own pretty little hands." I held them out and they were neither pretty nor clean. But I looked Padraic over with satisfaction—he did look mighty fine in his new green plaid vest. "The tweed is from Magee's of Donegal. I managed to purchase the very last piece of it."

"Not ever?! Why that's the finest there is." He lifted my hand and brought it to his mouth for a kiss. "I thank you kindly, my darling Brigid. I hope I can serve you well in this new vest."

"Well, it's just that you needed it badly," I said, not wanting to hear him go on so. "Now get out of here and let me finish up the cleaning."

By the time I washed the dishes, watered the horses, and got some dough rising for bread in the morning, I was tired to my bones. The light was falling from the sky and Padraic was nowhere to be found. I didn't know where he might have gone off to. Smoky was in the standing corral so he hadn't gone for a ride. Maybe just a long walk and a think. It was clear that Ella's passing had shaken him, too.

I crawled under the covers of my narrow bed and stretched to get comfortable. Suddenly, it felt like I was falling into rushing water, so overwhelming was sleep. I sank and sank until I was too deep. I was drowning and I couldn't breathe. I struggled to get out of the water, thrashing around to find a way to the surface. When I opened my eyes, hands were holding me down and I was screaming.

"Brigid, my Brigid, it's only me." Padraic had a hold of me and was talking gentle, like I was an animal that needed to be quieted.

"I was underwater. I tried to get out," I told him.

He leaned in and stroked my hair. "Sure and you're fine now. I have you. You're safe."

I could feel the fear leave my body as he held me and rocked me in his arms. "Oh, Paddy. What're we going to do?"

He kissed my forehead. "About what, my love?"

"About everything."

"We don't need to worry about anything now." He bent over me and his mouth found mine. The kiss was powerful, and again I felt like I was drowning, but this time I wanted it. I wanted to be swept away. I lifted up the covers so he could come in with me.

"Are you sure?" he asked as he slipped his body in next to mine. His warmth was such a comfort.

"As sure as I am about anything." Which means not much, I thought to myself. I took his hand and kissed his palm. He nuzzled my neck and then slipped his arms around me. I put my head on his chest so I could hear his heartbeat. And I fell asleep again.

23

I woke to an empty bed. Padraic was gone from my side.

As I dressed I could hear him outside the soddy, whistling an old Irish tune, one I had heard before but couldn't remember the name of. He sounded happy.

When I stepped out the door, he handed me a cup of coffee and gave me a wink.

"Thanks," I said.

"You better today?"

"What do you mean by that?" I bristled slightly.

"You know."

"I'm fine." I decided it was time to change the subject. I wasn't sure how I felt about what had happened last night, and I didn't want to talk about it. "I'm going back over to Ella's."

He dropped the piece of wood he had been carrying and shook his head. "Brigid, leave it be."

"I just want to see that Ella's been taken away and check to see if I can find anything useful at her house. Maybe she left a note. Maybe there will be some evidence of who did this to her."

Padraic looked at me and snorted. "Maybe you're sticking your nose where it don't belong. Don't you learn? There's plenty we need to be doing around here without you going off again."

Now he was just looking for excuses to keep me from going, and I would not take that from him. "I think I've been doing my share around here—cooking the meals, washing your clothes, trying to make this place livable," I said.

"I'm not saying you're not. But you're just going to get all upset again, and I don't want you to be like that."

He had a point. I could be a bear when I was upset. When I felt unhappy I often wanted others around me to be unhappy, too. Unfortunately, with my silver tongue, as my mam used to call it, I could make that happen.

"Padraic, I'm sorry I've been short with you. I just can't feel settled until we know what happened to Ella. What if there's something over there that would tell us who killed her and why? You know the sheriff isn't going to go looking for anything."

He moved in close to me, took me gently by the shoulders, tipped my head up so I was forced to look at him. "We might never know. It is not your fault that she was killed, and it's not your responsibility to find the culprits."

He had put his finger right on the problem, and I squirmed under his gaze. "But what if—"

Padraic broke in. "No buts. You can go over to Ella's and nose around, but then come back and try to settle down and help me get some work done. Who knows? Seamus might be showing up anytime now. We want this place to be looking as good as it can."

"You're right. I won't take long, and I'll help you when I get back. I promise."

"Fine and all, but you know there is no greater fraud than a promise not kept."

"Oh, Lord, Paddy, now you sound like my father."

"He probably couldn't get you to behave neither."

✻ ✻ ✻

I saddled up Grian and we trotted off quite nicely. I was trying to ride her every day, and she was getting ever easier to handle. Even her gait was smoothing out now, so it was a pleasure to sit on her back.

I don't know what I expected to find at Ella's, but I needed to have a look and see if anything I found helped make sense of her death. And if she had a family I could write to and give them the sad news. I hated to think that nobody would care that she had died.

When I rode over a rise, I could see that there was a horse tied up outside Ella's house. Could I have been wrong about the sheriff, and he had come out himself to take a look-see around? I pulled Grian to a stop and slid off her, tying her to a nearby tree. I patted her nose to quiet her and walked quietly down the hill toward the house.

As I came around the side and looked in the window, I could see a man bent over, looking through her things. When he stood up and turned, I saw that it was Bart. He had been digging through a trunk that sat at the end of the bed.

I stood still, hands pressed against the glass and watched him, wondering what he was looking for so feverishly—money? I picked up a branch that was lying by the house—a piece big enough to defend myself with—and walked to the open door.

When my shadow took away the light, Bart turned toward me. "What?" he yelled in surprise. His voice quavered and I saw that he was more afraid of me than I was of him. I dropped the branch and entered the room.

The way Bart looked at me reminded me of how he had cowered when Ella was hitting him with the spoon. He was a gnarled-looking sort of man, everything was rather crooked on him, and he was thin as a rail. His hair was long and greasy, and his beard was as thin as a paintbrush. What had Ella seen in him?

"What're you doing here and what are you looking for?" I asked as I stepped closer to him.

"Ella put the deed for this place in her things. I just was making sure it was safe." He sputtered out. Then he drew himself up and said in a stronger voice, "Besides, this is part my place and I have every right to be here."

"But Ella—" I started to say.

He drew himself up and interrupted me. "Where is that woman? Have you seen her? I need to talk to her."

It took me a second to register that he didn't know she was dead. I decided to go along with him for a while. "Why?"

"We've been thinking about selling up, and I think it's getting to be time. I might have an offer," he said, giving me what he thought was a smile but was more of a grimace.

I stepped toward him and he backed away from me as I tried to talk to him. "But Ella doesn't want to sell the place. I know that for a fact. She told me her plans for getting more cattle. She loves it here."

"Yeah, but maybe she loves me more. She might change her mind. I am very close to persuading her."

I couldn't lead him on anymore. It was too hard. I had to tell him what had happened. "I'm sorry to have to tell you this, Bart, but Ella's gone. By that I mean she's dead."

My words hit him like a bullet. He crumpled onto the bed. "No! What're you saying?"

"I'm so sorry, but it is true. I found her myself down by that big old cottonwood tree."

"How?" he asked, pushing himself upright.

"What?"

"How did she die?"

"You sure you don't know?"

"I would not hurt Ella. She and me were doing all right together. Why would I kill her? Tell me how she died."

I gave in to his pleading. "I found her hanging from that cottonwood tree. And she didn't do it to herself."

He looked down at the floor, shaking his head and mumbling, "He did it. He said he would. Damnation, he killed her."

"Who, Bart?" I pushed him.

He looked at me, the color draining from his face, and staggered toward the door. "It's not my fault."

"I'm not saying it is. But tell me who did it? You know who is responsible for this?" I wanted to shake the answer out of him.

"I can't say. Please don't ask me."

I could see how scared he was, his hands clenched together, his face screwed up something fearful.

"Then it will be the sheriff asking you," I told him.

With my words he turned and ran out of the house. For a moment I thought of chasing him and trying to get the name out of him, but he scrambled on his horse and took off before he was even in the saddle. So I stood in the doorway and watched him ride toward town. I knew it might be the last time I saw him.

I felt certain that he hadn't been part of Ella's hanging, but equally sure that he knew who had been behind it all. And that he was scared to death.

* * *

Entering the house, I had a feeling Bart would return for whatever he had been searching for. In the meantime, I'd have a look around, go through Ella's belongings, and see if I could find anything worth her life. I stood in the middle of what had been her home and looked around. Her lovely big bed, the curtains she must have made, the dishes put away on shelves: this life she had put together was over.

I took myself to task and started looking through the trunk, mostly finding blankets and sheets. At the bottom there were a few books and I was sore tempted to take them, but I thought better of it. Below them were some papers and letters.

I opened a sheet of paper and saw it was the homestead deed like the one we had been given. It had only Ella's full name on it, Ella Bates: not Bart's. So she owned this place outright. But maybe her husband could claim it if he heard of her death—and surely he would. For a moment I thought of taking it, but it didn't seem like the right thing to do. I already felt like I was trespassing on her life.

There were letters from her family. I pocketed the one with her mother's name on it so that I might write her and tell her of her daughter's passing. That would not be an easy missive to write.

Then I found one with just her name scrawled across the envelope. I opened it and read:

Ella,

I'm coming to get you. I finished with the railroad, and we can finally settle down together. Last I heard you were in Cheyenne, so I'll go there. Send word if you can to the post office. But I'll find you no matter what. Don't you worry, sweetheart. Things will be just fine. See you soon.

Your husband, Willy

The letter was postmarked a month ago. I wondered if he had found her.

I wondered if I could find him now.

I rode back to our homestead at a gallop, anxious to tell Padraic all I had learned. I hoped now he would see how important it was that we do something about Ella's death.

It felt good to give Grian her head, letting her run as fast as she wanted to, until now something I hadn't dared to do. She was young and energetic, so a little freedom would do her good. I loved the feeling of the wind rushing by, the surge of her muscles under me straining and pulling, the sense that I had control of this six-shooter horse. That's what they called a mighty fast horse.

I came into our yard at full speed, then pulled her up short and quick. But Padraic paid no attention. He was over by the door of the soddy talking with some cowboy. His attire told me he was part of a cattle outfit. With his broad-brimmed Stetson, his high-heeled boots, and his woolly chaps, what else could he be?

Then the cowboy turned and took off his hat and waved at me. I almost jumped off my horse. Grabbing the pommel, I dropped the reins and slid out of the saddle. A man with red hair and freckles was calling my name.

"Seamus!" I yelled and ran into his arms.

He hugged me, then twirled me around.

"Finally," I gasped when he put me down.

"Brigid, you're here."

"Yes, I suppose Paddy has told you all our news." I was a bit disappointed because I wanted to see Seamus learn he was about to become a well-off gentleman from the sale of the mine.

"He told me how you got this homestead. That Tom Dyer is one nice man. Sure and that's grand."

I looked at Paddy, and he smiled and shook his head.

"You don't know about us selling the mine?"

"Well, I figured we must have got something."

"More than that." I asked, "Do you know what happened to Billy?"

"He's not here?"

So Paddy hadn't told him much.

"I think we need to be sitting down for this. It's a long story," I said as Paddy pulled out the boxes and the one chair around our table, which was still outside.

At the same time Seamus brought out several bottles of beer. "Thought we might need these."

When we were all comfortable, Paddy nodded at me. "It's your story to tell, Brigid. I thought he needed to hear it from the horse's mouth."

"Oh, so I'm a horse now," I flung back at him.

But I turned somber as I recounted what had happened since we had last seen Seamus—how I had figured out who had killed Lily, that both Billy and Charlie had their hands in the doing of it. And what had happened at the mine when Billy fell down a shaft to his death.

Seamus shook his head. "Sure and I'm sorry to hear Billy's fate. He was a good lad and all."

"He was," I agreed.

Then I went on to tell about the last meeting with Mr. Hunt and how I had bargained him into giving us more money than he wanted to and even more than we had hoped.

"Well, where is this money?" Seamus asked, looking around. "I see little evidence of it here."

Paddy stepped in and told him how Mr. Hunt had sent the money order in all their names. That we had gone to the office but we hadn't been able to touch it until he came back and could sign for it too.

"So that explains why you were so happy to see me."

"*Begorrah*, Seamus. How can you say that? You know that's never true." The joy of having my own brother teasing me again made me laugh so hard I almost fell off my box.

"Let's go now," Seamus said, jumping up.

"Settle down, cowboy. It will still be there tomorrow." Paddy pushed him back into his chair.

"Yes, Seamus, tell us all that you've been up to. What were you doing for so long out on the range?" I asked him.

I couldn't take my eyes away from this man who was my brother, like I was studying him. He had changed fair enough—his hair was longer, his face was burnt and freckled, his hands were rough and covered with scrapes. "You look like you've been through a war."

"You could say that again. It's hard work this roping and branding. The calves are shy of us and quick. I've been grassed a time or two, trying to manage one."

"Grassed?"

"Toppled off my horse."

Seamus took a long swig of his beer, then dove in to telling us about life out on the range, the other cowboys, the chuck wagon, the bedrolls, the wolves, the cattle. Even when he was complaining, he was smiling and chuckling about what he had been through. "Yup, it sure puts a man to the test. It'll be good to have a day or two off."

I looked at him, surprised. "But you're not going to keep doing that, now that we're here, are you?"

"I don't know. Haven't thought about it. What have you got to offer?"

Padraic laughed and said, "A bed made of grass, a roof over your head, and a creek down the way."

"Not bad," Seamus agreed.

"And the chance to make something of ourselves," Padraic said seriously, "turn this into a ranch and run a head of cattle. Be your own boss."

"You think?" Seamus asked.

"Why not? If those others can do it, why not us? Look what we came away with in Deadwood. Let's take that money and make some more."

"It's harder than you think to start out. And the big sugars don't like the newcomers. They call people that have a small homestead 'nesters,' and they try to run them out, take over their land."

"But you've already got an in with this Bothwell. Wouldn't he be willing to help us out?"

"That I doubt. He's a fair-enough boss, but he's looking out for himself. That's how he got to where he is. What do you think, Brigid?" Seamus asked me.

I didn't want to tell him of my doubts right away. "I think we've got a lot to think about, and we don't have to figure it all out right now. We can get our money, fix this place up a bit, and see what we all want to do."

Seamus laughed. "Same old Brigid. Always the level-headed one. But, hey, that was some pretty fancy riding you were doing on that sweet little palomino. If Da could only see you now."

I shoved his arm. "And you, with your high-heeled boots and your shaggy pants. He wouldn't know what to think."

"What? Don't you like my *chaparreras*? Otherwise known as chaps. They're the latest fashion on the range. This is what I came over here for, to be ridiculed." Seamus looked me up and down. "I notice you've got yourself a nice new hat. Where'd you get it? Steal it off a cowboy?"

I took my hat off and swatted Seamus with it. "I need it to keep the sun off my face and brush away flies."

"Well, we'll take you shopping when we get our money."

"I can take myself shopping with my share of it. It's split three ways, now that Billy's gone. That's what Padraic and I decided."

Seamus turned and looked askance at Padraic. Padraic leaned forward and slammed his beer bottle on the table. "Brigid got us more money than we would have even have thought to ask for. She's more than earned her share."

Seamus chuckled. "This is what happens when I'm not around to manage things. Watch out: she'll take over everything."

"You'll be lucky if I even stick around," I threatened, knowing there was some truth to it. Then I added, "And what's this business about your new name, Jimmy me boy? When we asked for Seamus, no one knew who we were talking about."

It was hard to tell if he was blushing, but he hung his head for a moment, then said, "The fellas just started calling me that. I sorta like it. Makes me sound more like the rest of the outfit."

"I suppose I'll go from Padraic to Pat," Padraic said.

"Not by me," I said. "You two will always be Padraic and Seamus."

"Is it all right if I bed down here tonight? I brought my bedroll, and from what I can see of your place, it's a good thing I did."

"Of course, you must stay. This is your home too," I told him.

"So tomorrow Paddy and I will get up and go into town to claim our money and celebrate," Seamus said.

"I'm going too. I have other things to take care of, and I've already signed it," I told them. "Also, I want to check to see if someone's doing a funeral for Ella."

"Who's Ella?" Seamus asked. "And why is she having a funeral?"

So I told him the sad story of our neighbor's demise. When I finished, I noticed he was looking at Padraic. Padraic gave him a glance and shook his head.

"Who knows? Maybe she deserved it," Seamus said.

I couldn't believe my own brother would say such a thing. "No one deserves such an end, and certainly not a woman. And I think I might know who had something to do with it." Then I told them about my encounter with Bart the scrawny. "He as much as told me he knows who did this to Ella. But before I could force the name out of him, he took off. I am going to find him when we're in town. And I'll be looking for Ella's husband too."

Padraic rolled his eyes and looked skyward, saying, "I tried to tell her, Seamus. I knew I shouldn't have let you go over there by yourself."

Seamus stood up and stared down at me. "Brigid, enough of this. You need to stop this sniffing around. It will bring nothing but trouble."

"Someone has to do it."

"But I'd rather it was not you. Please, for the love of Jaysus, leave it be." Seamus shook his head. "My sister, give her a silver star, she thinks she's a sheriff."

25

It was a late night for all of us. Even after we finally went to bed, we'd fall quiet for a moment or two, and then Seamus or Padraic would think of something else they had to tell each other, and we'd be off again, talking and laughing as the night sky filled with a million stars. I blessed each one of them for bringing my brother back to me. The comfort of having Seamus in the same room with me was better than words can say. He lay stretched out on the floor between Padraic and myself. He snuggled down into his bedroll, which consisted of a horse blanket on the bottom, a wool blanket on top with a quilt, which he called a "soogan," covering it all. When Padraic tried to give him his bed, Seamus had insisted he was comfortable on the ground and that he was happy to have a roof over his head.

I said my prayers softly to myself and then listened in delight as a gentle snore arose from Seamus. He hadn't changed that much.

*　*　*

I woke to the smell of coffee brewing and two empty beds. How had they managed to get up and leave me sleeping? Not that it wasn't appreciated. I dressed quickly and joined them at the table outside. The day was turning warm, and it felt good to be sitting in the sun.

"Well, she's finally arisen. May I say, dear sister of mine, that you are looking stunning this morning." Seamus stood as I sat down and swept a bow my way. He had always been so theatrical.

"Actually what I feel is stunned. You're here and we're all together. Can it be too good to be true?" I asked.

"More goodness to come when we get our loot." Seamus stood and fetched a mug for me. "Would you like a cup of *jamoka*?"

I looked up at him smiling down at me and gave him a puzzled look. "You've learned some awfully odd words from your new companions—*loot, jamoka*. What would our mam be thinking?"

That stopped Seamus, and I was sorry I had mentioned Mother. She had died this past year since we had left Ireland. It was a great sadness to us both that we had not been there with her. When we first left our country we had hoped we might return someday, but now we knew we would never see her again.

Seamus handed me my mug and said, "Wait until you hear me swearing. I've learned some great cussing. There's nothing like a cowboy who's been tossed from his horse for coming up with some real wingdingers."

Padraic almost spit out his coffee laughing so hard. "You'll have to teach them to me so I can fit in."

We all laughed at that. It seemed to me that since Seamus had returned, there was a new ease between Padraic and me. For one thing, we hadn't talked about what had happened between us the other night, and now we might not have a chance or a need to, which was fine with me. I liked the feeling of just being where we were and not having to try to figure out what anything meant or where we might be headed.

"You ready to saddle up?" Seamus asked me.

"Let me first finish my coffee and my toilette."

"You look fine to me," he said.

"But we're going into town, and what's good enough for out here will certainly not do for the big city of Cheyenne."

Just to teach them a lesson about trying to rush me, I took extra time and care with getting ready. First, for my coiffeur, I brushed out my hair and then pinned it up into a chignon. I put a touch of rouge on my cheeks and lips, then topped it all off with my new somewhat fancy hat, my town hat. When I finally stepped out of the soddy, the boys were waiting for me and had thoughtfully saddled up my horse. I was happy climbing on the saddle and sitting with my legs on either side in my split skirt. As soon as I was seated, Padraic and Seamus let out a yelp and slapped their horses into a gallop. Grian had no intention of being left behind as she gave a leap and bolted into a gallop after them. I would have flipped off backwards if I hadn't been gripping the pommel of the saddle.

Maybe life wouldn't always be easier with Seamus back. The men did seem to rile up each other. I guessed it was the price I'd pay for their company.

❀   ❀   ❀

Once in town we split up, agreeing to meet at Dyer's Hotel in an hour or so. In high spirits they went off to collect our money. Since I had already signed for it, I didn't have to be there, and they had promised to bring me to take care of my share. We had decided we each would receive fifteen thousand dollars, and we would put the remaining five thousand in a fund to use to fix up our homestead. I told them to bring me only a hundred dollars in cash and put the rest in an account under my name. I didn't want to know what they would do with their money; I assumed most of it would go toward cattle. But if they wanted to go wild with some of it, that was fine too.

In the meantime I went to the church that the undertaker told me was handling Ella's funeral. It was a Baptist church, and I wasn't sure how one was supposed to behave. There was no holy water by the entrance so I walked in slowly and did a small genuflect just in case that was appropriate. A woman was putting flowers by the altar but she hadn't heard me. I walked over and asked her about the funeral.

"I think there's to be one tomorrow. Some poor woman who broke her neck. You should talk to the pastor."

Or had it broken for her, I thought, wondering how the story was getting around. "Thanks much. Where might I find him?"

She pointed to a door to the side of the lectern. "Through there, then his office is the door to the left."

I was expecting an old, bent-over, wispy-haired gentleman, but who I found was Pastor Lehrke. He introduced himself as he ushered me into his office. He was tall and standing up military straight, his blond hair tucked behind his ears and his bright blue eyes clear and far-seeing. I put his age at maybe ten years older than I.

"I'm Brigid Reardon," I said.

He looked quizzical, then said, "Please take a seat."

"Oh, I won't be staying. I'm Catholic." Now, why had I said that?

"How may I help you?" he asked, taking his place behind a large wooden desk with a globe on one side and a pile of papers on the other.

I decided I might as well sit down, so I slid into the chair he had offered. "I'm a friend of Ella Bates. I didn't know her long or well, but she was my neighbor. And I wanted to know when the funeral was to be and if I could be of any help."

"That's mighty kind of you, Miss Reardon. I think it will be a small affair. She was not well known in the county. In fact, I only met her once or twice myself. We're planning it for two o'clock tomorrow afternoon, and you're more than welcome to attend."

A small affair—I wondered what that might mean. In Ireland, everyone came to a funeral, both to pay their respects and to eat the fine spread and drink that would be served afterwards. "Should I bring something to share?"

"To share?" he asked.

"Would you be having a gathering afterward?"

"No, we don't take to doing anything like that. Especially since she was so little known. It will only be a short service and then to the cemetery."

"Oh, that's all?" It seemed to me that once again Ella was getting mistreated, as if she weren't good enough to be cared about.

"I'm sure it will be enough for the few people who will come. I'm glad you will be one of them. So you live out by the creek?"

"Yes, we took over the homestead of a poor Irish man whose wife had died. He went back east with his children."

"I think I've heard of him, but he wasn't in my congregation."

"No, I don't suppose. Because he was Irish and all."

"But are all Irish Catholics?" he asked.

"All the true ones are. The Protestants aren't really Irish, they're English, and they have brought their religion with them, but it hasn't taken over."

"Well, let me just say that I will be happy to see you tomorrow and any other time you'd like to come and try out our church."

"I thank you for that, but I'm happy how I am." I stood up. "I will see you tomorrow with my brother and my friend."

He stopped me as I was at the door, grabbing my wrist and turning me about. "I forget myself. I'm sorry I didn't say this sooner, but I'm so sorry about what happened to Miss Bates."

"Yes, it was I who found her." He was still holding my hand.

"This is beyond belief, that a woman should be treated like this."

"You mean killed," I said clearly.

At my words, he dropped my hand and shook his head from discomfort. "Yes. Whatever she'd done, she didn't deserve to be murdered."

"She'd made the mistake of trying to claim a homestead and make a living like a man would. Some man didn't like that. So he took her life." I turned on my heels and left the room.

*   *   *

I hadn't told Padraic, because he thought I stuck my nose into too many things, but there was another thing I wanted to check on. I had to know how the boy whose foot had been shot off was doing. I remembered the doctor's office where the boy had been taken and found it easily, just down from the Mercantile. A brass plate next to the door read DR. HOFFSTEIN. I knocked and a gravelly voice told me to enter.

In his office I found him hunched over his desk working on something. I was glad that I had found him alone and not with a patient. He looked up when I entered and pulled his glasses down from where they had been perched on his head. The doctor was an older man—I judged him to be in his late fifties. He looked tired and I could tell that he was trying to place me.

"I know I should know you," he said. "Let me see. Might you be a patient of mine?"

"No, I was with the men who brought in that poor boy who had been shot in the foot."

"Ah, yes." I could see that he now remembered me from the incident. He waved his hand at a chair in front of his desk and so I sat.

"I wanted to know how he was doing."

The doctor wiped at his face, then shook his head sadly. "There was nothing I could do for his foot except remove the rest of it to his ankle. It was beyond salvaging. Now the worry is gangrene. I was a doctor in the rebellion, the Civil War, whatever you want to call it, and I saw too much of that damned infection, pardon my language." He paused, remembering what he had been through.

I had certainly heard much about this war between the states, but it happened before I had arrived in New York. For that matter, it had occurred before I was even born.

Dr. Hoffstein went on: "I cleaned the wound as best I could and I told him how to care for it. But he'll never really recover from it. It's a horrible shame, that shooting, just horrible."

I agreed. "Actually it's worse than that. Not a shame, but I call it a sin. Do you know where the boy has gone?"

"I sent him to the frontier hospital—the new one's being built yet— and I hope they have let him remain there, convalescing. It's going to take him time to get used to crutches and all."

I was still taking in the fact that the boy's foot had been cut off. I wondered how he would go on with his life, what he would be able to do out here on the frontier. I sat still, wishing it weren't so.

The doctor cleared his throat. "I'm sorry you had to witness such an event, and you such a young girl."

In truth, I didn't feel that young. "All I can say is I never want to see anything like it again. But I was glad to be there to comfort him."

"I know it helped him."

"But what will help him now?"

The doctor shook his head and looked down at his hands. "I would have a lot fewer patients if those cowboys would put away their guns when they come to town. There's no sense to the shooting that goes on around here."

I stood, seeing that I was keeping the doctor from his work. I tried to think of something uplifting to say, but there was nothing. "Do you know what has happened to the men who did it?"

"Oh, I doubt that they've come to anything. Too much of that kind of thing goes on in this town."

"But surely the sheriff would want to find out who was responsible for injuring that boy."

"Ma'am, it don't work like that out here." The doctor shook his head slowly and then said, "In Cheyenne, people are pretty much on their own. We've only had a sheriff for a few years."

"So you see a lot of the results of such gun fights."

"Too many," he sighed.

"Well, I'm going to talk to the sheriff. At least it will make me feel better, whatever comes of it."

The doctor stood up and looked at me like he wanted to tell me something more.

"Yes, go on," I encouraged.

Finally he said, "The sheriff might do something if he knew who they were, but who even knows who they are? Not that I blame the sheriff, he's kept busy by all the ruckus that goes on around here."

At his words, I remembered the red-bearded man with the feathers in his hat. "I will find out."

26

The entryway into the tent where the doctor had told me the boy was staying was merely a flap pushed back. In front of me were two rows of cots with six men to a side. Most were sleeping, one was leaning over the edge of his cot coughing. At the far end I saw the small form that I guessed might be the boy I was looking for. I walked carefully and quietly down the aisle, but the men still noticed me. One waved, one whistled.

When I got to the foot of the boy's cot, I stood for a moment and watched him sleep. He was sweating although it wasn't that warm in the tent. I hoped he wasn't running a fever. As I looked down the length of his body, I couldn't help notice that the heavy woolen blanket caved in where his one foot had been.

"Lookie what we got here," a man yelled from the next cot over.

The boy opened an eye and then shook his head. He propped himself up on one elbow and stared at me. "I thought you were an angel," he whispered.

"Not hardly that," I told him and walked closer to his side so our conversation could be more private.

"You were the lady who helped me, yes?" He tried to lean up on one elbow, but I could see that moving pained him, so I gently pushed him back down.

"I did what I could," I murmured, trying to erase the picture of the shooting in my mind.

"If it weren't for you, I think they might have finished me off," he said rather matter-of-factly.

I found it hard to think what could have happened to him, but it had not gone that way, bad enough as it was. "Who were they?"

"Just two cowpokes that bedded down near me. One was Jake and I think the other's name was Willy."

Willy, how common a name could that be? I wondered. "Are you sure?"

"Sure I'm sure."

"Do you know which one was the redhead?"

"I think it was Willy."

"Do you know his last name?"

"Never knew it."

"What do you know about him?" I asked a little impatiently.

"Not much. He showed up about a week ago, looking for trouble." With that the boy looked down at his legs. "I guess he found it."

I knelt by his bedside and said, "I'm Brigid Reardon. What's your name?"

"Brigid. That's a funny name. I'm Joshua Williams, but everyone just calls me Josh."

"How old are you?" I couldn't keep myself from asking. I figured he was a little younger than I.

"I'll be fourteen this year. What about you?"

"I'm after turning eighteen."

"You seem older than that."

"So do you." I smiled at him. He was a big lad for his age. "Well, Josh, I just wanted to check on you and see how you were doing. Has the sheriff come to talk to you?"

"What for?"

"Why, to find out who did this to you."

"That's not going to happen. They don't care about such things as the squabbles between us cowboys. If they did they'd never get anything else done."

"What happened to you was hardly a squabble. They could have killed you. Don't you want to see those men brought to justice?" I asked, not believing what he was telling me.

He shrugged, then winced. "Don't make no never mind. This place here is better than where I was staying, and nothing's going to bring my foot back. That's gone forever."

"What will you do?" I asked, wishing somehow I could take care of him. I wondered where his people were. "Do you have any family close by? I could get in touch with them."

"Nah. I left them long ago. Came out here to make my fortune, and I don't even know where they might be. I can take care of myself."

"But what of your foot?"

"The doctor said they could make me a new one. He told me they've gotten pretty good at it since the war and a foot isn't so hard to replace."

Again, I was surprised by the calm with which he spoke. "How's your pain?" I asked.

"No, they give me something for that. Makes me sleep most of the time. But you're worth waking up for." He smiled.

The pain medications he was being given were most probably the cause of his languid composure. While Josh might not care to punish the men who had hunted him down, I wasn't going to let them go so easily. "Where were you staying when you ran into these two men?"

"Why do you want to know that?"

"I might have a word with those two myself."

"Now, don't you go do that. They're not to be messed with, as you can surely see. They're nasty ones." But even though he had warned me off, he gave me the name of a boarding house, Rollins House, that was not too far down the street.

"Thanks, Josh. I'll watch myself."

"If you go there, would you tell the lady that I'll be back for my things?" Josh asked me.

"I'll surely do that."

As I turned to go, he reached out and grabbed my hand. "Come again if you can."

"I will. I promise." And I meant it.

❋   ❋   ❋

Next stop was the post office, where Willy Bates had said he would leave word for Ella. I was mailing off two letters—one to Ella's family and one to my own. As I walked over I wondered how long it would take my short missive to reach Ireland. I knew all too well the path it would take, having come out that way myself, but now there was a railroad that would carry it to the East much faster than I had traveled.

There was talk of a real structure being built for the post office, but at present it was occupying a tent. The counter of the office consisted of a wooden plank held up by two barrels. A man dressed like a cowboy with his hat firmly affixed to his head was working behind the plank, digging through a pigeon-holed cabinet. I could see that he was sporting a gun belt. I guessed it was all just part of the outfit, although people did send money through the mail and so he actually might need to use it.

There were two gentlemen ahead of me, carrying large packages. All the men in the office were wearing their hats, again just part of the way things were done out here in the West. No one had the manners to take off their hats when they entered an establishment. I waited my turn and listened to them talk about the weather and the sheep that were moving in on the range.

"Those measly critters could be the ruin of us," said one.

"The problem is they eat the grass, roots and all. Nothing grows where they've been. They'll be turning the plains into a desert," the other added. "It'll be the end of the cattle ranches. Mark my words."

"I dunno. There's talk of running those dang shepherds out of the county," the first man patted his firearm as he made this statement. "Might not be a bad idea."

"Long as they take their sheep with them."

Once they had gone, I handed my family's letter to the postal clerk who stamped it for a dollar and put it in a pile. "How long will that take?" I asked.

He picked the letter back up and read the address. "Going to Ireland. Should be there in a few months. It's the passage over the ocean that takes the time. It will reach New York in a week or so."

"Also, I was told that a Mr. Bates, Willy Bates, would leave a message for me here."

"Yup, but a young woman already came to collect it." He gave me a stare. "What do you want it for?"

"Yes, I know, that was Ella." I thought of telling him she had been killed but in the end didn't see the need so I just said, "But I need to talk to him, and I was wondering if you could tell me where he had been staying."

"Far as I know he's still staying at that bunkhouse down the street. You can't miss it right on the corner."

"Thanks very much." I turned away with this piece of information. I was right in my thinking about Willy. He had been staying at the same place that Josh had been staying—and his assailants.

27

"Don't tell me you're married to him too," the man who answered my knock at the door at the bunkhouse said, looking me over. "Another one already came asking about him."

"No, I'm not sure I've ever met the fellow," I told him in a clear, sure voice. "But I still want to find him."

"Well, he ain't here, but I wouldn't be surprised if he was imbibing down at the cantina 'cross the way."

The last thing I wanted to do was to accuse a man of murdering his wife in a saloon after he'd been drinking for a while. I wasn't that naïve. But I decided to go over there to at least get a look at him—to see if he was who I was thinking he was—and figure out what to do next about him. I peeked into the saloon, but there was nothing to it. I had to walk into the room if I wanted to be able to see all the men gathered in there. It was a dark, gloomy room filled with smoke. I couldn't help notice that the one other woman in the place was poised above the bar in a large full-length painting lying on her side, stark naked. I lowered my gaze as soon as I saw her. I also knew that it was not proper for a woman to enter a saloon, but I pulled my hat down low and figured it was early in the day and I could chance it. Also, who was going to call me out about it?

The noise in the place did drop down a bit as I stood looking around, but when I continued to just stand by the door, the men went back to their jawing. I was almost ready to leave when I saw a man in the back with feathers sticking up out of the band on his hat.

I walked a few steps in and came to the end of the bar. The bartender walked down and asked me what he could get for me.

"Do you know that man over there with the feathers in his hat?" I asked, nodding my head toward the back.

"Wish I didn't. He's nothing but trouble."

"How so?"

"Drinks too much, then starts to shove people around."

"Do you know who he is?"

"I think his name is Bates. He just showed up a week or so ago. Claims he's coming into some money and I hope so, 'cause he's sure spending it. I'd steer clear of him if I were you."

"I would, except I need to have a word with him."

"Well, you just take care."

I thanked him and then leaned against the bar rail, wondering what I should do next.

I turned back to the bartender and asked him, "Do you think you might tell him a lady wishes to speak with him and that he should meet me outside? If he seems resistant, tell him it's about Ella."

"If you say so," he said, shaking his head.

I turned and went back out to the sidewalk. I had a niggling feeling and decided I shouldn't let Bates out of my sight, so I stood by the window and watched as the bartender approached him. He stood up to talk to the bartender and I got a better look at him. Yes, I was sure now that he was also the man who had mercilessly shot the boy in the foot. The least I could do was let the sheriff know about that, even if I didn't think it worth my time to mention his relation to Ella. But I certainly needed to talk to him.

Then I watched as Bates turned, and instead of walking toward the swinging doors at the front of the saloon he moved toward the back. I realized there must be another exit and he was trying to avoid me. Without thinking, I ran down the alley to catch him as he came out the door. When he pushed the door open and saw me, I was sure he was going to push right past me too. But he stopped and took a good look at me. I saw his hand move toward the gun that was strapped to his thigh. "What'd you want with Ella?" he asked.

"You know she's dead."

He bowed his head. "I had heard something like that."

"Do you know anything about what happened to her?"

"What would I know?"

"I just wondered if you had any idea how or why she was killed. Seeing as you had gone out there to her place."

"Lookee here, Ella was my wife. She left me some time ago, but I was hoping we'd hitch up again. I had nothing to do with what happened to her. I wouldn't have hurt her. Why would I?"

His voice broke and I found myself believing him. He stood in front of me looking the figure of a dissolute man, one who did seem unhappy that Ella had died. But I wasn't going to let him off so easy. He had more to answer for. "Because you do have something to gain from her death. And you're about the only one who does."

"What would that be?"

"Her homestead. She'd been working it long enough that she owned it outright. And as her husband you would own part of it and would inherit her share. I would say that might be a good reason to get rid of her. For her land."

"I didn't care about that. I sure didn't want to settle down and try to run some cattle on it. That's not in my blood. Too much work. There's better ways of earning a living. Besides, I wouldn't hurt a flea."

Then I couldn't help myself. I had to bring up the boy. "I beg to differ. I watched you shoot the foot off a poor young lad."

He stared at me and nodded. "You were there. I remember you now."

"You got that right. I saw it all. You shot that boy when he was running away from you."

"Well, he got what he deserved," Willy said, then continued, "You're new around here. Maybe you don't know how things work. He stole something from me. Can't do that out here. We don't stand for it."

"I wonder if the sheriff will feel the same way when I tell him where you are," I said as I turned to go. He moved toward me so fast I had no time to react. He launched himself and grabbed me around the shoulders, then slid one hand up to my neck. I was facing away from him and could feel by the pressure he was applying to my throat that he meant business.

I remembered what my da had told me to do if a man ever grabbed me. "Go limp," he had said. "Let them think that you are not going to fight them. It will cause them to loosen their grip a bit. This is when you must act."

I let all my limbs go loose and dropped down in his arms. When I did this, he had to try to keep me from falling and to keep himself upright. That's when his arm slipped up by my face. I knew what to do. His arm was nice and close to my mouth. I opened my jaw wide and bit him as hard as I could. Even though my brothers always yelled at me when I wanted to be rid of them, calling me a cheating girl, biting had always served me well. He let out a screech and flung his arms out. I slid down to the ground but kept my eyes on his gun. I kicked at him with my foot and connected with his leg. He yelled and bent over to grab me.

Luckily his gun was almost staring me in the face. I reached up and plucked it out of the holster, then jumped back and onto my feet. He grabbed my dress and I felt the fabric rip as he tried to pull me closer. I whipped away as fast as I could, not caring what happened to the dress. I stumbled, almost falling, then whirled around, facing him. I pointed the gun in his direction and hoped I wouldn't have to use it.

"Now, wait a minute," he said as he scrambled backward. "Don't go pointing that thing at me."

"You're not going anywhere," I told him. "So stop moving."

"Listen. I didn't mean you no harm. Put the gun down or it might go off," he whined and backed up another foot.

I kept the revolver pointed at his chest and he stopped moving. I heard a noise behind me but didn't turn my head. The bartender came barreling through the door and stopped when he saw I had a gun on Bates. "You all right?" he asked, his voice rising. "What's going on here? I was watching out for you."

"I saw him trying to run away, so I came after him."

"I told you he's not to be trusted."

"I'm fine now," I told him. "Why don't you run and get the sheriff? I think Mr. Bates has a few things he'd like to tell him."

Just then Mr. Bates decided he didn't like the way things were turning out and decided he'd better skedaddle. He turned and took a step away, but I couldn't let that happen. I aimed the gun down and let off a shot. It pinged the ground right next to his boot and stopped him in his tracks.

"What do you think you are doing? Don't shoot," he yelled. "Geez, you almost hit me."

The bartender threw his head back and laughed. "I guess you do know what you're doing."

"Yes, and I came close to shooting you on purpose. To let you know how it feels. But I wasn't about to follow in your footsteps and lame you for life. Now just settle down and wait for the sheriff and you'll be fine, Willy."

He was shaking, but he turned back toward me and stood his ground. "You don't know what you're doing."

"I think I do. But if you want to find out, try that again."

28

Sheriff Sharples handcuffed Mr. Bates even before asking any questions, which I thought was right smart of him. After he had Willy secured, I felt comfortable lowering the revolver I'd been holding and handing it over to the sheriff.

The sheriff looked at me and asked, "Now, Miss Reardon, what's this all about? I've got this fella cuffed, but you need to give me a reason why I should take him off to the jail."

I had been thinking about what I would say while I kept my gun leveled at Willy Bates and had decided I would not bring up the possibility that he had had anything to do with Ella's murder. But I hoped that what I would tell the sheriff would certainly be enough to keep Willy locked up for a while.

"Willy Bates came after me, that's for sure. Even ask the bartender." I nodded at the bartender who was standing watching the proceedings. "And now to hear that he was the one who shot off a poor lad's foot while he was lying in the street. And it was for almost no reason at all."

Willy broke in. "That's not so. I had a damn good reason. He stole from me and I was just trying to get back my possession. If he would have stopped running, we could have sorted it out civil-like, but he wouldn't stop so I shot at him. I was just trying to scare him, but he ran faster than I thought and it hit him in the foot."

The sheriff looked at me. "That wasn't how it looked to me," I said. "You were gunning for him and he had fallen down. Sheriff, I was an eyewitness." The sheriff nodded but didn't say anything, which was good because I wasn't finished. "Let's start with what he had done. All the poor boy did was try to get warm in the night, and he borrowed one of your blankets to that end. You took his foot off over a blanket."

Willy shrugged and said, "I wasn't sure he hadn't taken more, like some of my money."

I didn't want to argue that point as I was ready to move on to what he had tried to do to me and almost succeeded. "And then, when I tried to have, as you like to call it, a civil conversation with you, you grabbed me and threatened me."

"No, that wasn't what I was doing. I was just trying to get you to stop. I wasn't going to hurt you none." When he said this, he looked down at the ground. He couldn't even look me in the eye.

"It was plenty clear to me that you were set on strangling me." I turned to the sheriff. "He had his hands around my neck and was choking me."

"Yeah, but you bit me. You fight like a girl," Willy spit out.

"I use what God gave me. It was only because I managed to grab your gun that I'm here to tell of it at all."

The sheriff turned to me and asked, "Did anyone else see what happened between you two out here?"

The bartender stepped forward. "I saw most of it. She asked me to tell this fella to meet her out the front for a talk, but instead I watched him slip out the back door. She saw what he had done and went after him. I was worried when she didn't come back, so I came out to check on her. When I found the two of them, she had his gun."

The sheriff looked at Willy. "What do you have to say about that?"

Willy squirmed and then lashed out. "It was all her fault. I didn't know what she was going to try to do. She comes out here accusing me of things and I just was trying to get away from her when she grabbed my gun. If anyone is at fault here, it's her."

❋ ❋ ❋

The sheriff, as I hoped, took my word and the bartender's word for what had happened and marched Willy Bates off to the jail, pointing Willy's own gun at him. He let me go when I promised to come by before I left town and sign a statement telling what had happened. When I finished my shopping I went to the jail and found the sheriff sitting out front, talking to another man.

"You locked him up?" I asked.

"Here's the young lady who defended herself by biting her attacker," he told the other man. "Quite a good defense." They both started hooting at the thought of it.

"Whatever's at hand," I told him, not joining in their laughter, "I had hoped to talk to him."

"I think you two have had enough interaction today. Let him be. You'll be safe enough with him inside."

"Yes, but he might also be involved in Ella Bates's death. He was her husband and had more than an opportunity."

"That so?" The sheriff looked thoughtful. "I'll take that up with him, but you need to stay out of it. What you can do is make a statement."

29

After I had signed my statement, the sheriff took hold of my hand and, like a father, said, "I want you to watch yourself. There's many a rough crowd around here, and that episode with Mr. Bates could have turned out badly. Steer clear of sticking your nose into things." I tried to look demur and agree with him, but then I had to ask him if he had found out anything about what happened to Ella.

"That's what I mean. I'm going to let Bates sit in the cell for a while before I start to ask him questions. You leave it to me."

I hoped he would figure out what happened soon so I could leave it be.

✻ ✻ ✻

I was to meet Seamus and Paddy at Dyer's Hotel when I was through with my errands. I knew exactly where I would find them. Sure and there they were, sidled up to the bar with their heads together, probably planning some new venture for our land. I stood in the entrance for a moment or two just to enjoy seeing them both there. Some good must come of this, the three of us back together again. A bit of home for me.

Walking over to meet them, I had decided I would wait a bit to tell them what had transpired between Willy Bates and myself. I had checked myself over in a storefront window to make sure I didn't look too disheveled. Stories told a fair time after the fact weren't as disturbing, I had found. There was no need to stir the two of them up over something I had already taken care of—but I would be happy to tell them that Willy Bates was behind bars. And I hoped that with my brother around, Paddy wouldn't feel so burdened with watching over me.

At first, when I appeared at their elbows they looked surprised to see me. Almost as if they had been caught at something. Then there was nothing for it, but they would order me a beer of the kind they were having. A beer might be just what I needed to calm down after my ordeal and to celebrate again my brother's return and the influx of cash from the payment of the mine.

And then there was the money. I think the fact that we had gotten fifty thousand dollars for the mine had finally registered with Seamus when he got to hold some of it in his hands. I wondered how long it would be before he spent a goodly amount of it: my dear brother was not the most cautious when it came to money.

"I feel like a king right now," Seamus laughed and showed me a roll of bills. "Or, since we're on this side of the ocean, a president. No royalty allowed here."

"You take care with flashing that cash around," I warned him. "Some fancy woman's going to see it and decide she likes the look of it." As if on cue, who should wander in but Miss Molly. This didn't surprise me at all. Like a hound on the scene she always seemed to know when Paddy was near. She was not in her waitress uniform and looked a pretty picture indeed. I tried to be glad to see her.

I knew that Molly got free room and board while she was working at the hotel. This explained how she could be so well turned out all the time: she had the extra money to spend on her clothes. Today she was dressed in a light summer frock with lace at the neck and sleeves. The cream color of the dress made her blonde hair, pulled back into a chignon, even lighter.

"My brother has finally returned!" I exclaimed. "Seamus, this is Molly—she works at the hotel." I took note of the fact that Seamus stood up somewhat straighter as he was introduced to her.

"Hello, Seamus." Molly smiled at him and gave him her hand. He took it awkwardly as if he wasn't quite sure what to do with it. He gave it a light shake and that seemed to suffice. She continued to smile and then said, "You must be right happy to be back with your brother and sister."

Seamus laughed and said, "My sister, yes, it's grand to see her. But what brother is this? I love Padraic like a brother, but this here fella is no brother of mine."

Dead silence.

Molly tightened her lips and the smallest "Oh" came out of her mouth. She turned and looked at Paddy, then at me. "So then, you two are not related?" she inquired.

I squirmed. The lie had been told so innocently and then we had become caught up in it. Now was the time to come clean.

"It was because—" I started at the same time that Padraic stammered, "You see we thought . . ."

I shut up and Padraic continued, "It was just easier that way, with everything, you know." He held out his hands in a form of supplication.

"I see," Molly said, but she didn't look like she did see. She looked like she was put out by our behavior. "And now I'm to believe that this handsome fella is really a brother of one of you."

"What's this all about then?" Seamus demanded. "To be sure, Brigid and I have the same ma and da. Both of us Reardons. What have these two been telling you?"

Molly shook her head and seemed quite bewildered by what she had learned. "It will take me a while to sort it all out. But it is nice to meet you, Seamus, and I'm sure I'll see you all again. I must be off."

Paddy stepped forward and touched her arm. "We meant no harm. 'Twas so awkward the two of us traveling together, don't you see? I'm sorry we didn't tell you the truth earlier. Stay for a time and have a drink with us."

"Not today. I have some errands I must take care of."

I could tell Paddy was put out by her refusal. "We've news to tell. There's been a murder out our way, and Brigid was the one to find it."

"Oh, I had heard of it. A woman, they say."

"Yes, our neighbor, Ella Bates."

Molly's eyes flashed. "What has this town come to when they're now hanging women? We might have the right to vote, but they still don't like to see us getting ahead in the world."

"Her funeral is tomorrow," I said, then added, hoping to placate her, "Molly, why don't you join us there?"

She considered this for a moment, then looked at me and said, "Yes, that would be a right thing to do. I will let others know. We should show our concern for this horrible act."

30

My two lovely men had done a fair bit of shopping in town, and when we got home they cooked up a feast for us: steaks over the open fire, a fine loaf of bread, potatoes cooked over the coals, and a bottle of red wine that I knew was a good one because I had seen it when I worked for the Hunts. We sat outside and ate as the sun colored the clouds the soft hue of heather.

"I haven't eaten this well in a long time," said Seamus. "I ate more beans out on the trail than I care to think about."

"Lord, sleeping on the ground and eating beans—what a life! You must feel like our little soddy is a palace," I teased him.

He grabbed a hank of my hair and tugged on it, but not hard. "You watch it: you'll be bunking down in the corral with the horses."

"Probably make less noise than you do at night," I came back with, while giving him a sweet smile.

"Do I have to sit between you two?" Paddy asked, laughing. Then he pulled out a small bag and handed it to me. "Sweets for the sweet."

I could smell the delight before I even saw the label. The sweet dark smell of chocolate. Paddy had brought me a bag of cocoa; he knew well my great weakness for this hot drink. I ran into the house to get a small pan to make us all a treat.

While I carefully stirred some of the cocoa with water and sugar over the fire, the two men talked about what they wanted to do with the homestead. They were both very excited because they had talked to Seamus's boss, Albert Bothwell, about buying cattle from him. Seamus explained how the cattle just had free range over the plains all summer, which was why they needed to be branded. This saved a huge amount of money that they didn't need for feed.

The two of them had a long talk about what their brand should look like. Seamus was all for something traditional like a star or a moon with a line above or below it, while Padraic thought they should design their own. Padraic suggested a backwards *R* for Reardon combined with a forward *P* for his first name. He drew it out in the dirt with a stick, and I thought it quite nice—simple and easy to read. Seamus reluctantly nodded and said that might be fine, but he didn't look like he was going to agree so easily.

"Where do you put the brand?" I asked, trying to head off a fight.

"Right on their flank," Seamus slapped his thigh.

"How?"

"You heat up the old branding iron in the fire, throw the young'un down, and press it into their hide."

"Does it hurt them?" I couldn't help wonder.

"Hardly at all. Their hide is pretty thick."

"Where will we put all these animals that you're going to buy and brand?" I asked, looking out at the corral that was just large enough for our three horses.

"Listen, Brigid, there's money to be made in this business. We don't need to worry where to put them. They won't be here but for passing through," Seamus said when he saw my grimace.

"Wouldn't we need a bigger corral?"

"Down the road. So we build one. You need to trust me on this. I should know. I watched Bothwell sell his steers for between fifty and sixty dollars a head. And it costs almost nothing to raise them as they live off the range. I'm telling you, we take some of that money we got from the gold mine and buy a herd of, say, a hundred cattle, and we'll more than quadruple it by next year. It's a sure thing."

I never quite believed it when someone said it was a sure thing. There were just too many things that could go wrong, many of them events one couldn't even imagine. But I decided not to say anything to diminish their enthusiasm. We were having such a nice dinner, no need to spoil it with practicalities. Besides, Seamus seemed to know what he was talking about. After all, he had been working in the business and knew what was involved with such an endeavor.

"If you say so," I conceded, but I did wonder how I would fit in. I thought about them off riding the range while I stayed alone in the soddy. I didn't like what I envisioned for myself—stuck at home and feeding them when they were around. This was not the life I had imagined. But again, I decided I didn't need to bring up such issues on our first real night together.

※　※　※

When we were done with our dinner, Seamus surprisingly offered to clean up. Maybe the time on the range had taught him to do his share of the chores. "You two go off now. Take a walk this fine evening."

The moon was coming up over the horizon and looked like a glowing coal in the darkening sky. I was glad not to be stuck in the house doing chores. Paddy offered me his hand as we headed down toward the creek. We walked in silence for a while, but the feeling between us was warm and good. When we reached the banks of the creek, we stood on a large rock and watched the water flow below us.

"Brigid, you're quiet tonight," he said.

"Just enjoying the evening. Thanks for that wonderful dinner. And the cocoa. You mustn't spoil me."

"I wish I could." He squeezed the hand he was still holding even though there was no need for it.

"It's grand to have him here, is it not?" he asked me. "I know how you've missed your brother."

"Yes, but it's rather odd. I've missed him badly, and yet now that he's here it feels like it was always so."

"Oh, you two will be wrangling like you started to do today." Paddy pulled me toward him as if to capture me.

"Watch out or it will be you I'm wrangling with." I pulled out of his embrace, but not too far. Then he turned and lifted me up in his arms and twirled me around like I weighed nothing.

"What was that for?" I asked when he set me back down.

"Brigid, I have another little something for you that I got in town." He reached into his pocket and pulled out a small packet but didn't hand it to me. Instead, he took me by the shoulders and made me look him in the eyes. "I know you've been waiting on me, but I, too, thought your brother should be here before we settled on anything," he explained. "I knew you felt the same way and I honor that."

"Yes," I said, half-worried about what he would say next.

"I think it's time we marry. Enough of being brother and sister. What do you say to that?"

He looked so expectant it stopped me. Here it was—the proposal that I had been waiting for. It felt so ordinary and expected, like he already knew the answer.

I stood silent for a moment. This was what I had wanted for a long while, and yet now that he had asked me to marry him I felt unsure. All the talk of the cattle and the plains and the life out here, I couldn't help feeling overwhelmed. At the same time I knew I couldn't put Padraic off any longer. This was the way it was meant to be. What was I thinking?

"Yes, I think you're right," I told him.

"So now's the time to open this." He handed me the packet.

I opened it and found a golden Claddagh ring, two hands holding a heart with a crown on top. It was the traditional engagement ring in Ireland, but I hadn't expected to see one here.

"Oh, Paddy. It's lovely. Wherever did you find such a thing out here in the wilderness?"

"It's made from a piece of gold from our mine. I had it made for you at a jeweler's here in town."

"Would you be kind enough to slip it on my finger?" I offered him the ring and my left hand. He took it awkwardly. "You remember how the ring must sit?" I asked him, thinking he might not. "The tip of the heart should point toward the fingertips—this will mean we're engaged. When we marry, I will turn it the other way around."

He shook slightly as he tried to put it on my hand. I hoped that it would fit my finger. With all the hard work I'd been doing, my hand had grown rough and thickened. I reached down and helped him wiggle it on.

"May I?" he asked as he leaned in toward me.

"Oh, this time you ask," I teased him. But the words had scarcely left my mouth when his lips were on mine. There was no river holding us up this time, just our two bodies merging to become one, but we managed to stay upright. The kiss went on for a time as we explored how to do it together.

While I thought I knew the shape and size of Padraic, I was surprised by his heft. Feeling his arms around me and myself pressed against his chest, I felt the weight of him as if I were holding a wild animal. He was like to eat me up. It was both scary and emboldening. He kissed me and squeezed me until I thought I might not breathe again. But I was learning to kiss him back with equal fervor.

Then he moved his hands from my shoulders down to my breasts, and I both liked the feel of it and wasn't ready to give in to all it meant. I gave him a moment, then gently pushed his hands away. As we finally broke apart, I could tell he wanted more. "Soon," I whispered as he laid an arm around my shoulders.

"Oh my Brigid, not soon enough," he whispered back and gave me a gentler kiss. "Who do we have to answer to? We're as good as married now, and it's a lovely evening."

"We should get back," I said.

"Seamus wouldn't mind," he suggested. "He probably thinks we've already been together in that way."

"He does not." I hoped that wasn't true.

Once more Padraic gathered me in his arms and kissed me with such great warmth and tenderness I thought I would melt into him. But finally I was able to gently push him away.

"Maybe Seamus wouldn't, but I would mind," I insisted. "This is not how I want it to be. We've held off for so long, let's wait 'til we are married."

Part IV

The Funeral

Oh, beat the drum slowly and play the fife lowly,
Play the Dead March as you carry me along:
Take me to the green valley, there lay the sod o'er me,
For I'm a young cowboy and I know I've done wrong.

—*Cowboy Songs*

31

The next morning, as we dressed for the funeral, Padraic put on his vest to wear for the first time. Seamus admired it and gave me the best compliment, saying that not even Mam could have sewed it better.

"What did he do to deserve that fine vest?" he asked.

"Stayed with me and didn't get into trouble, like some men I know."

"And for that he deserves a kiss," Padraic said as he moved in close and gave me a light kiss on the mouth. "Fits like a glove," he crowed when he backed up to show it off. "And good with the pockets. You know a man can never have too many pockets out in this dangerous country."

"I'm glad you're going to wear it to the funeral."

"Yes, indeed. This is for my very best occasions. I certainly won't be wearing this fine garment to herd cattle." He smoothed his hands down the front of it and looked quite pleased.

"I'll make you another that's not quite so fine for your chores," I assured him.

He grabbed me around the waist and squeezed me. "What a fine wife you're going to make me."

I couldn't help wonder about that. What kind of wife might I be? And what kind did he expect me to be?

✻ ✻ ✻

Later that day we met Molly and some of her friends outside the church, even though Padraic put up quite a fuss about not wanting to go, saying he didn't even know the woman. "Seamus didn't either," I pointed out. I had insisted that he and Seamus attend the funeral—both because I didn't want to go alone and because I didn't think that there would be many people there. I felt that Ella deserved better.

Molly had brought along a woman friend, and she introduced her as Redelia Clark. She added, "We worked on getting women the right to vote. We went on the marches together. She even spoke to the legislature. When I told her what had happened to Ella, she wanted to come along to bear witness to her death."

Redelia spoke right up. "This is intolerable what happened to that poor woman. This is the first time I've heard of a woman being hung in Wyoming, and I hope by God that it's the last." We all agreed and walked into the church to a slow hymn being played on the organ in the back. A woman was singing along with the music, "Abide with me, fast falls the eventide." I had heard the song before but did not know it well enough to join her in singing.

Unfortunately, I was right about the number of people who would attend the service. Besides the six of us, there were only a handful of men and women who sat scattered among the pews. I didn't see either of the men in her life—so I surmised that the sheriff had kept Willy locked up and that maybe Bart had decided to make himself scarce as he seemed to know more than was good for him. But I had hoped Bart would show up and I could try to talk him into telling me what he knew about Ella's murder. I was determined to get him to tell me what he knew, for I was certain the sheriff wouldn't track him down.

It surprised me all over again when the pastor began to speak in English, not Latin, but I had to remind myself I was not in a Roman Catholic church. While it was nice to understand what was being said, for me it took some of the mystery out of the mass and made it seem more commonplace. The service was quite short with no communion, and when it was over we walked outside and stood on the sidewalk to talk.

Redelia took my arm and said, "You know what the daily paper has written about her, don't you?"

I shook my head. "We just got to town. I haven't seen the paper yet. Do tell me what it said."

"This article claimed she was a low woman, probably a prostitute. It went on to state that she was rustling cattle from Bothwell. They made it sound like she deserved what she got."

"I don't believe a word of that," I blurted out, even though I hadn't known Ella that well or that long.

"Well, I'll tell you this," Redelia continued. "The *Cheyenne Leader* is right in the pocket of the stock growers' association. It prints what they tell it to print. It claimed that she had rounded up a whole herd of mavericks from the range and was getting ready to sell them in the fall."

"So it's against the law to take mavericks?"

"Because they haven't been branded I guess they could be considered fair game. Not unusual for someone else to grab them if they're close by their herd, but it's certainly frowned upon. However, such an act is not usually considered a good enough reason to kill someone."

"I'm glad to know they're calling it a murder. That's what it has always looked like to me."

"I suppose if she took a lot of mavericks, it could have stirred up the cattle barons something terrible." Redelia shook her head. "They might well have taken the law into their own hands."

"Well, I was over to Ella's homestead, and I didn't see but a handful of cattle in the corral. Not anything like a herd," I said as I thought back to my visit. "Do you think I should go and tell the sheriff that?"

Padraic touched my arm and said, "You've already done what you could. Isn't it bad enough you had to find her?"

"I'm afraid that it probably wouldn't make a mite of difference," Redelia said. "Many men here think that women are only a step above the heifers. You should have seen how some of them treated us when we were asking for the vote."

Molly joined in the conversation. "Some of them would even spit at us when we did go and vote. It gets worse. Three years after they gave it to us, they tried to take it away, but the governor put an end to that."

Redelia added, "That wasn't true of all of them. After all, enough of them voted for us that we did get the vote. It does no good to lump them all together. But I do think that many of these cattle barons think they own the town."

"Bothwell isn't as bad as some make him out to be." Seamus joined in the conversation. "Why, he even gave some of us a bonus for the good work we did when we came off the plains, but I admit he does lord it over a person."

Molly sidled up to Padraic. Looking up at him with a smile, she asked, "Would you all like to join us for some refreshments at the hotel?" He looked ready to consider this suggestion, but I didn't want to be around her any more than I had to be, glad as I was that she had come to the funeral and brought a friend. Maybe, sometime, we could all be friends.

I touched my ring and wondered if Molly had noticed it. I knew that Padraic had not had time to say anything to her about our engagement—even if he wanted to inform her. I would show it to her in my own good time. But not now. I decided it was time to step in.

"Thanks for the invite, but we have to be going," I said. "Seamus is still getting settled, and we have much to do at our place."

Molly took a step back as if I had insulted her. "Of course. I'm sure you are all very busy. I hope that you enjoy having your brother back. It must give you some peace of mind."

Not to be outdone by her show of kindness, I said, "It was so good of you all to come to Ella's funeral. I thank you for that."

The truth was I wanted to get home and then go over to Ella's and see if I could catch Bart before he left for good.

32

We didn't get back to our place until late afternoon. The sky was filling with castle-sized dark-gray clouds that were swirling up a storm. When Padraic and Seamus had finished taking the gear off their horses, they went into the house for a drink. All I wanted to do was to join them, but I had one more mission to accomplish on this sad day. Since they were so opposed to my investigating Ella's murder, I told them I was just going to take Grian for a ride.

"Be quick about it," Padraic said. "It's looking like it's going to storm, which would be good 'cuz we need the rain."

"Always need the rain out here," Seamus added as they walked toward the house. "The boys say it's as dry as a bone long bleached."

I watched them head into the house, then swung back up into Grian's saddle. I hoped the rain would wait.

❋　❋　❋

I stopped at the creek and let my horse have a good, long drink, but then I gave Grian her head and let her stretch out into a gallop. I loved the feel of her long, ropy muscles rolling under the saddle and the wind pulling at my clothes. I loved seeing the land from horseback; the wider view showed its beauty while close up you walked in dust. We made good time over to Ella's.

The corral was empty. As far as I could see there were no horses or cattle anywhere near the house. If Ella had in fact stolen any cattle, they had already been removed from her premises. I wondered what had happened to them. Could it be that whoever was responsible for her death had come back to claim them? Maybe that was even why she was killed, but it seemed like such an unlikely response. Couldn't they just have ridden in and taken the livestock and let her live? Why did they have to kill Ella? To punish her and take her herd. Surely not for such a small herd of cattle. There must be something more to this murder.

I reined in Grian right up close to the front door of the house, trying to hear if I could make out if someone was in there. Other than a few flies buzzing around, the place seemed dead quiet. I feared that I was too late to get anything out of Bart. He had probably lit out for some other town. I didn't really blame him—what was there left for him in this place after Ella was gone?

I swung myself down from the saddle and wrapped the reins around the post that was near the front of the house.

"Hallo," I yelled so as not to startle anyone. No answer back.

I pulled open the door and peered inside, but it was too dark to see much. As I stepped in I saw that the place had been turned upside down. Dishes smashed, coverlets torn, the mattress pulled off the bed. From my visit I knew that Ella was a decent housekeeper. This mess was far worse than she would have ever kept it.

One more step in and my eyes adjusted to the lack of light. I looked down and saw a hand sticking out from under the table. I gasped and then was shocked at the sound of my intake of breath. I leaned over to see what or whom the arm was attached to. It was poor Bart. He was curled up like a child with that one arm flung out and the other held close to his face.

All I could figure was that he was dead drunk. Or so I hoped.

But as I leaned closer and studied his face, I almost didn't recognize him because it was so contorted. He looked as if he was trying to scream. I reached down and touched his wrist. Cold as the water in a fresh spring. I pushed my fingertips into his flesh and could feel no response, no pulse, no life. I put my finger by his nose and felt no air moving. Quickly, I pulled my hand away and backed up.

I was too late. He too was dead. Now Bart would never tell anyone what he knew. How had he died? And why? Because of something he knew? I had to guess that was the reason. Had both he and Ella been killed for the same reason? Cattle? Money? Revenge? The way the house was torn up told me that whoever did this had been looking for something.

On the table was a bottle of whisky and three glasses. Two were empty and one had a slightly blue residue in the bottom of the glass. Certainly not the color of whiskey—something much more potent. I was afraid I knew what Bart had drank—arsenic. Either he had done it unsuspecting what was in the whisky or he had been forced to do it. The blue color told me this. For the past few years, arsenic was being colored blue so people would not take it by accident. One could get the poison almost anywhere—a pharmacy, a hardware store—for vermin and the like. If I knew Ella, she probably had some close at hand, as did most homesteaders, to keep the rats away.

I hoped Bart's death had been swift and that whoever had done it was far away by now. I knelt down by him and made the sign of the cross. No matter what faith he might have been, it couldn't hurt. I said a short prayer: "Hour of grace, our hour of death, this hour is good by God's will and by Mary's." Then I gently reached over and closed his eyes. I could do no more.

✻ ✻ ✻

As I was giving the house one more going over, I heard the sky split apart. A bolt of lightning cracked so close at first I was afraid it had hit the house. Then I feared for my horse. I ran to the door just in time to see Grian rearing up and pulling at her reins. Another bolt of lightning slashed down from above, and she broke free and was gone before I could stop her. There was no running after her—I would get drenched and she would stay far out of my reach.

I pulled up a chair and sat in the doorway, watching the rain come teeming down. If only I had told Paddy and Seamus where I was going or, better yet, had one of them accompany me. I hoped Grian would go home and they would come searching for me. She knew her way.

I decided to make use of this time and see if I could find anything useful in Ella's house. Two books by the bed caught my eye. If nothing else I could take them home. I knew Ella wouldn't begrudge me them.

One was of course the Bible. Seemed like there wasn't a house to be found in America that didn't have such a book. I knew most of the stories already, but I took it to have at hand. The other book looked more interesting. It had a red cover with writing in gold that declared it one of the Knickerbocker books—*The Leavenworth Case,* written by a woman, Anna Katharine Green. I wondered what the case could be about, so I opened it to the first page and read: "I had been a junior partner in the firm of Veeley, Carr & Raymond, attorneys and counselors at law, for about a year, when one morning, in the temporary absence of both Mr. Veeley and Mr. Carr, there came into our office a young man whose whole appearance was so indicative of haste and agitation that I involuntarily rose as he approached, and advanced to meet him."

I skipped down the page to learn that a Mr. Leavenworth had been murdered, "shot in the head by some unknown person while sitting at his library table." I wanted to keep sitting right there and read it. The case in question was therefore a murder investigation. I sat back on my heels and thought, but this is good news. This book, while not only being intriguing, might actually give me some help solving the murder I was looking into. I could hardly believe my good luck to have found such a useful book.

I turned back to the Bible and opened it to see if Ella had written anything in it. Her name was written in black ink on the inside cover and a date, 1854. She must have been given it as a present when she was young. Maybe for her first communion or whatever they did in her faith.

And now she was dead. I shivered at the thought and also at the thrashing of the storm outside the house. I wanted to be back safe with my men.

I looked up and Grian was standing by the steps. She appeared thoroughly drenched with water running off her back. I walked out and grabbed the reins, pulling her in closer to me.

"You could have gotten hurt. You could have gotten tripped up with the reins and broken a leg. I could have lost you." I scolded her.

She nickered at me and shook water.

"But you're a good girl. Thanks for coming back for me."

The storm had abated, which I was thankful for. I knew I had one more task to do before I returned home. I needed to take one more ride into town to tell the sheriff I had found another body.

33

After I dried off at home, I knew I had to ride into town to tell the sheriff what I had found at Ella's. Seamus and Padraic were nowhere to be seen, or I would have sent them. At least the rain had stopped when I saddled up Grian again. She looked back at me and nickered as if to say, Here we go again.

When I got to the jail I was glad to find that the sheriff still had Willy locked up in a cell. But this meant that Willy probably couldn't have had anything to do with Bart's death. I was back to square one. When I told the sheriff about finding Bart dead on the floor of Ella's house, he gave me a wide-eyed look, then said, "You are getting awful good at finding dead people. Tell me why this might be?"

As long as he asked me, I would tell him what I thought. "This is what I surmise: that the two deaths are connected. The only reason that I happened to have found Ella was that she was a friend and our neighbor. And I went there again to talk to Bart. I guessed he was camped out there. He knew something about Ella's death that he wasn't telling. So there you have it."

The sheriff scratched his chin and looked at me sideways. "I'll send the doctor and coroner out to check out this latest death."

"I'm afraid Bart might have been poisoned," I told him.

"Now, dash burn it, why would you think that?" He seemed to be getting mad at me. Was it a case of kill the messenger? I didn't want to find out.

"Because there was no bullet hole and he didn't look beat up. And there were glasses on the table."

"Could have been one of them heart attacks," the sheriff suggested.

"I don't think so. There was a tinge of blue in the glass. I'm guessing arsenic." I hadn't touched any of the glasses so the coroner could see what I had seen.

"Well, thankee for coming in with this news. Now I need to attend to this," he said as he turned away from me.

I was so tempted to try to talk to Willy, but it just didn't seem like the right time. The sheriff was in a foul mood, and I had plenty of other things to take care of back at the homestead. "Let me know what they find," I said.

The sheriff whipped around. "Are you still here? You'll find out the news like everyone else. Probably in the paper."

"Is the coroner Dr. Hoffstein?"

"Matter of fact, he is."

"All right then."

"Listen, Missy, you stay out of this. Whoever is behind these deaths is not fooling around. Much as you're an irritation, I'd a soon not see you dead."

❀   ❀   ❀

When I got back to the homestead, my two cowboys were busy smoking cheroots and drinking beer, their feet up on boxes and their hats pulled down low. I couldn't even imagine what I looked like having ridden all the way into town and back.

"There she be," Seamus said. "I told you not to worry. My Brigid always finds her way home." They looked so happy I hated to tell them more bad news.

"My but you both look comfortable and lazy," I told them instead. "I, on the other hand, had to do more than find my way home. No thanks to either of you. Probably weren't even worried about me."

"If you'd stick around here once in a while, you'd see all the hard work we've been doing," Padraic said slowly, and I could tell he was trying to put the fire of my anger out before it started blazing. "Seamus and me, we're planning on building a barn next to the corral. We've been pacing it out and clearing out the brush. Next we'll start digging the foundation."

Somehow this news surprised me. I knew they planned on getting a herd of cattle, and if I had thought it out, I would have known that a barn would be needed, but there was part of me that hadn't stepped into this whole ranch deal yet. I wanted to say, Wait a minute, I'm not sure yet. But I knew it wasn't up to me. They had barely consulted me about their plans. Now that Seamus was in the picture, Padraic hadn't talked to me much at all about his plans.

I looked down at the ring on my finger. Except for this. I twisted it and tugged at it, wondering if it wasn't a bit too tight. Maybe it was stuck on and I could never remove it.

"Oh, and your wish is going to come true tomorrow night," Padraic said, lifting his hat up into the air as if in celebration.

I wondered what he was talking about. I hoped he didn't think we'd be getting married that quickly. The banns hadn't even been read or anything to do with the priest. "What wish is that?"

"That fancy ranchers' club in town. As I recall you wanted to see the inside of that place."

"You mean the Cheyenne Club?"

"Yes, indeedy. We've all got an invite to have dinner there."

"How did that come about?" I asked.

"Mr. Bothwell was so pleased with my work that he invited me and the two of you to have dinner there Saturday night. It will be a good chance for us to quiz him on where and how to purchase some good stock. He might even give us a deal on some of his. Who knows."

This all took me by surprise. I wasn't too happy with what I had been learning about Bothwell, and I wasn't sure I had anything suitable to wear to such an evening, but I did so want to see how the club looked inside. Everyone said it was like a palace of some sort.

"But what will I wear?" I asked.

The two men burst out laughing and slapping their knees.

Seamus chortled, "I told you that's the first thing she'd say." Off they were again, laughing so hard that I thought they'd collapse. I wasn't so sure I at all liked the way they were ganging up on me.

I stamped my foot. "Well, you two might be thinking about that also. I'd be surprised if—between the two of you—you can even manage to find one decent outfit for such an evening." That stopped them for a moment.

Paddy said proudly, "I'll be wearing my new vest and will be dressed with the best of them."

Then Seamus stood up and put his hands under his suspenders, leaned back, and said, "I'll show up how I please."

"Not if I have anything to say about it," I said, then added, "If you'd stop laughing for a moment, I have some bad news."

That shut them up mighty fast. "What now?" Seamus asked. "Is it about that darn woman again?"

"Well, I wanted to check on the place, make sure everything was as it should be . . . but it wasn't at all." They both stared at me. "I found Bart dead under the table. I suspect poisoning, but the coroner's gone to check on him. I had to ride into town to tell the sheriff."

"Oh, Brigid, I'm so sorry," Padraic said and moved toward me.

I took a step back. Somehow I didn't want his comfort at that moment. I had more to say about what was happening. "They were our neighbors. Now they're both dead. And you two are thinking about staying here and building a barn and all. What kind of place is this, I ask you?"

"I think it's over now," Seamus said reassuringly. "Whatever this was about is probably finished."

I looked at him. "How can you be so sure?"

He shrugged. "Just a feeling."

Padraic nodded. "Maybe they brought it on themselves."

"Well, if they did, I'd certainly like to know how." I didn't like how the two of them were ganging up on me and trying to shut me up.

❀ ❀ ❀

Padraic found me cutting out the calico fabric for a suitable summer frock. I was bound and determined to look my best at this dinner. The last time I had worn a fancy dress was to a dance almost a year ago. I couldn't help remembering that I had been kidnapped during that dance. Afterward, I repaired the rips and washed the dress carefully, but I have to admit it had lost some of its shine, and in the end I got rid of it.

Padraic looked at the makings of the dress and then at me. "In that gown you'll be the belle of them all."

"Don't you try to sweet-talk me after the good time you've had laughing at my worries."

"It's Seamus that starts it, surely. Once he gets to laughing, there's no stopping him. You know this."

"What you don't seem to understand is that I'm having a hard time and don't appreciate being laughed at."

"Come here, my love." He came close and wrapped me in his arms and I recognized I did want to be there. In the heart of me I did trust him and knew that he would protect me if I needed it. But, for all that, his comforting didn't stop me from worrying about what might happen next out here on the plains. Like the thunderstorm that had just passed through, trouble seemed to boil up and pour over all of us.

34

The next day Dr. Hoffstein, the coroner, stopped at our homestead on his way back to town after dealing with Bart's body. I watched him walk toward the soddy, and it seemed to me he looked older than when I last saw him a day ago. Maybe caring for another dead body did that to a person. He told me that he had sent Bart's body off with his helpers on a wagon. Then he asked me with hardly a howdy-do, "How did you happen to stop by that house and find the body?"

I decided that just because he had no manners didn't mean I had to stoop to his level. "Please have a seat," I waved at our one chair. "Might I offer you something to drink?"

He looked me over, then shook his head. "Pardon me. I didn't mean to jump on you like that, but I forget my manners when I have to examine yet another dead body. They're not my favorite customers."

"I understand."

He gave me a wry look. "By gad, I bet you do. After all, I'm not forgetting that you're the young woman who helped the lad who was shot in the foot. It's Brigid, isn't it?"

"Yes, one and the same. It was lucky I was there to help the boy."

"I would not call that good luck to find two men in such states."

"No, but at least for the boy I could help. I was too late to do anything for Bart. He was stone cold."

"Yes, I'd say he had been dead close to a day. And now that you mention it, I wouldn't say no to a glass of water. It would be mighty appreciated." He sank into the chair and I ladled out a cup of water from the bucket.

I watched him as he swigged down the whole cup. "More?" I asked as he handed the glass back to me.

"That'll keep me going until I'm back in town and can drink some-thing stronger to soothe my nerves."

"What do you think happened to Bart?" I asked, after deciding not to tell him what I was guessing.

"Can't say for sure, but it looks to me like poison, most probably ar-senic, since it's so easy to get. But arsenic isn't a pleasant way to go, and I doubt he would have drunk it on purpose. My guess is that someone put it in his whiskey without him knowing it. Maybe they thought that way it would look like he died of a heart attack or some such natural occurrence and we'd not come looking for them."

I nodded. "I wondered when I saw the color of liquid left in the glass in front of him."

"Oh, so you knew as much. Yes, that did help me in my diagnosis." He gave me a stare. "Brigid, you're awful smart to be stuck out here on the prairie. How did this come to be?"

I wasn't quite sure how to answer that so I said, "It's a long story, and sometimes I'm not sure myself."

"Someday I'd like to hear it."

"Cheyenne is sure to grow and have more to offer, don't you think?" I asked.

He laughed. "You are an optimist, but probably right. If I were going to do it again, I'd probably settle in Salt Lake City."

"Salt Lake City? Why?"

"Well, it's just a bit farther down the railroad line. Might be hard to live there and not be Mormon, but I think things are much less dangerous there. For starters, they don't believe in drinking."

"Salt Lake City, huh. No drinking would probably help a lot."

"Much as I'd like to sit and talk with you, I do need to get to town and deal with this body. Did you know him? Why would someone do this to him?" the doctor asked, shaking his head.

"I don't have a clue what's going on, but you know that Ella was his partner out there on the claim. You handled her after she was killed."

"So I did. They didn't paint the nicest picture of her in the paper, but I don't care what kind of woman she was—an angel or a floozie—she didn't deserve what she got. It boils my blood that anyone would do that to a man, but somehow to a woman is even worse."

"I couldn't agree more. It was horrible finding her hanging there."

He shook his head and looked down at his feet. "There is much that I think is good about Cheyenne, but many of the folks who live here are a lawless bunch and don't think the rules apply to them. They come out to this wide-open country and think they can do whatever they please."

The word *lawless* struck a chord with me. I had been feeling that way about this territory, and I wasn't sure I could tolerate it.

"Well, Bart as much as said he knew something about how and why Ella was killed. He might have known who was responsible for her death and they decided to do away with him before he could tell anyone. To answer your first question about how I happened to find him—that's why I went over there. I was going to try to get the information out of him. Earlier he had suggested to me that he had an idea about who had killed her. But obviously, I was also too late to learn anything."

The doctor stood up and rested a hand on my shoulder. "Listen, little lady, you stay out of this. I don't want to have to come out here and find that you've been strung up too. These fellas are not to be messed with, and that's a fact. You let me and the sheriff do our jobs."

"I know you will, but do you think the sheriff will? I don't have a good feeling about him."

Dr. Hoffstein dropped his hands and said, "He'll try."

❊   ❊   ❊

A short time after the doctor left, another rider showed up. I was inside and just heard the clatter of hooves. When I stepped out, Molly was swinging down off her small filly. She had on a dark riding outfit with a split skirt. I envied her the handsomeness of her ensemble.

"To what do I owe this honor?" I said as I walked up and helped her tie her horse to a post.

"I just thought it was about time you and me had ourselves a little talk," she said as she pulled off a pair of leather gloves and slapped them together. She seemed like she wasn't very happy about something.

"Let me guess." I tried to lighten the mood. "You want to know if Seamus is really my brother."

"Sure, but what I'd really like to understand is what the real relationship with you and Paddy is. I noticed you've got a ring on your finger and I never saw it there before the other day. What does it mean?"

"I'm sorry," I started, even though I wasn't quite sure what I had to be sorry about. I twisted the ring, a habit I had acquired since I put it on. I wasn't accustomed to wearing anything on my hands. "It must be rather confusing, but Padraic and I have been half-engaged for a while now. I insisted that we not do anything until we had found my brother. So we claimed to be siblings, as we told you, to make life easier. But now, well, he gave me this ring the other night, and I'd guess you'd say that we're now formally engaged."

Molly blinked her eyes and slapped her gloves with a crack on the skirt of her dress. I was glad she wasn't using them on me. "Well, that's just dandy. Here I've been sniffing up to him, hoping that he might be interested in me, and come to find out that there was never any chance of that."

"I did notice."

"You could have said something, dropped me a hint to back away, even if it wasn't the truth."

"Yeah, I am truly sorry about that. I did get the idea that you liked him in that way, but again we were so accustomed to being siblings, I didn't think it would be good to change our story."

"Well, I'm not dumb, and I did wonder when I saw the way the two of you behaved when you were together. I'm glad I found out how things stand between you two before I did something really embarrassing."

"I know Padraic likes you, too."

"You don't have to say that. There's a lot of men in this town, and it isn't like I don't have my pick." I was sure that was true.

She wiped down her skirt to clear it of dust, then did a little sashay. "In fact there's to be a fancy dinner at the Cheyenne Club in a couple days, and I've already got me an invite."

I decided not to tell her we would be there, too. She seemed to need to feel good about something, and I wasn't going to ruin her gloating. At least I could let her have that.

Molly untied her horse and swung up on the saddle as her filly skittered around. When she had her settled, she said one last thing before she rode off. "One thing I know for sure is I'd be a better wife for Paddy than you'll ever be."

I watched her kick her horse into a gallop, kicking up dust as they headed away. She was a good rider, I'd give her that.

And I feared that her final words might be true.

35

Molly's visit took the stuffing out of me. I couldn't help comparing myself to her, and I didn't always feel like I came out ahead.

I looked around in the soddy and all I saw were things to do: I should spruce up my dress for the dinner at the Cheyenne Club, think of something to make for supper out of the odd assortment of food we had on hand, dress the beds such as they were, but instead I left the house and walked over to the corral to talk to Grian, who always seemed to understand me and not judge me.

"I might never know what happened to Ella," I told Grian, and even though there was a fly buzzing around her ear, when she shook her head I knew she agreed with me. "I thought I could find it out, but one of my two suspects is in jail already and the other is dead. So who could have killed her? I've no more suspects and have nowhere to go to find them."

Grian pawed the ground. I knew what she wanted. She thought it was time for a ride. She hadn't been out of the corral all day. I needed to get away from the homestead too. A good hard ride would lift me out of my doldrums, and maybe something would occur to me. It often happened that way—walk away from what I'm trying to figure out and the answer appears.

As I was saddling her up, I decided to go back to where I had found Ella swinging in the wind, the big cottonwood tree on the other side of the creek. I hadn't been there since that day, and I didn't want to be avoiding it as if the place itself were evil. Who knew, maybe something would strike me there, or maybe it would just be another way to say goodbye to Ella and begin to let go of the mystery of her death.

Grian was in a feisty mood, and so I gave her her head and let her run it out. No sense in fighting her energy. Once she had her gallop she would settle down and behave. Plus, I loved riding hard across the prairies, the wind combing through my hair, my eyes tearing up at the beauty of this land where I felt no sense of belonging. Would I ever feel at home here?

We made good time and soon I saw that tall cottonwood tree off in the distance. The large tree was letting loose of its cotton, and it floated and fell through the air like snow. When we were nearly beneath it, I pulled up Grian and knotted the reins and attached them to a bush. "No running off again—no matter what sound you hear."

As I stood under the tree, I looked up and made out the branch the rope had been hung from. When I looked down, I saw all the scuff marks left from when Ella had been killed and when she had been cut down. I hated to think of the fight she must have put up to keep from dying and of the fear that would have filled her. She would have fought even as she knew it was useless, because that was what Ella was like. Hard to imagine such a scene now, when the calm air was filled with white fluff and it was so quiet I could hear some small creature moving through the grass. The cotton seeds twirled and danced in the warm air. Someone had told me that the Indians used them to stuff pillows. It would take an awful lot of that fluff to stuff anything. I soaked in the quiet and remembered. Why had such a terrible act happened in this place? What had someone been so angry about? Or had it even been about anger?

I had been focusing on the two men in her life—Bart and Willy— both claiming to have loved her, both having a reason for wanting her dead, but now it seemed like neither of them could have done it. What was I not seeing? Was there another way to look at what had happened to her? I had been assuming that she was killed out of anger, but now I wondered if she might have been killed because of greed, what such sordid events were often about—money.

I hadn't really thought of that, because Ella had little to no money to spare. But what I had been overlooking was that she owned land. And her homestead was right on the creek, making it very desirable, as water was of major importance in this desert-dry land. So who wanted her land?

I found a large rock sticking out of the ground and made myself comfortable on its flat surface. I sat so still that a small bird came hopping along the ground, hunting bugs, I presumed. While I wasn't exactly sure what the bird was called here, I knew it was some kind of sparrow, for it looked similar to the ones we had in Ireland. In that moment I missed Ireland so deeply—a place where I knew the names of all the plants and all the animals and all my neighbors. Would I ever find that sense of belonging in this country?

The speckled bird hopped almost to my feet.

When I leaned in closer to get a good look, I startled it, for it flew a short distance away and then disappeared into a bush. Most all the plants in the plains were covered with thorns, which did not lead one to want to get too close to them. But out of curiosity, I wanted to see if I could find where it had gone and maybe make out the nest.

I walked over to the bush and bent over to inspect it. As I did the sparrow flew out the other side. I carefully grabbed two branches, avoiding the thorns, and moved them apart.

In the crook of a branch I could make out a small nest. I saw a flash of color and wondered if there were eggs in the bramble of sticks. Leaning in closer I could see that something was stuck on a twig near the nest. I reached in and pulled it out. A piece of wool fabric was what I held in my hand.

When I realized what I was holding, my heart started to pound. A piece of finely woven woolen fabric was in my hand, made into a tweed that I had come to know well, as I had sewn the vest for Padraic out of it— green with red and yellow threads making the plaid pattern in the weave. But I was sure that I had saved all the scraps from the vest, so this piece had not come from our homestead. Also, it appeared to be a pocket that had been torn off a coat. It had to have come from the one other person who I knew had purchased this tweed—and was probably ripped off in a struggle with a woman who did not want to have a rope put around her neck.

None other than Mr. Bothwell, the Big Sugar himself.

36

From far across the plains I could hear my two lads, Padraic and Seamus, whooping and hollering. As I rode up I saw that they were sitting in the shade of the soddy, drinking beer and laughing. Padraic was leaning back so far in the chair I was sure he would tip it over. Eager to join them and find out what they were celebrating, I quickly slid down from Grian's back and pulled off the saddle, throwing it over the top rail of the corral and then took her bridle off. I rubbed her nose and said I'd bring something special for her soon. She deserved a treat as much as all the rest of us. Speaking of which, I hoped there was a beer left for me.

"What's got you two so stirred up?" I asked, tempted to push Padraic that little bit farther off his stump and see him fall over.

"Hey, you're looking at the next two cattle barons of this fine spread," Seamus hollered. "We just bought our first herd. Five cows, and Mr. Bothwell gave us a very fair price on them. And he threw in an old gummer cow, who might still be able to have another calf or two." Hearing him say that name—Mr. Bothwell—gave me the shivers. I felt for the scrap of wool I had in my pocket. I wasn't sure if I was going to tell these two about my find and what I thought it meant. In some part of me, I wasn't sure that I could trust them to keep their mouths shut about it.

So instead I asked, "What's a gummer cow?" I have to confess I didn't like the sound of it at all.

"It's an old cow that doesn't have many teeth left," Seamus told me. "Has to just gum its food."

"Poor thing. Where are these cows?" I asked, looking around.

"Not here yet. Bothwell's keeping them until we're ready for them. We need to do some serious fencing work before we can bring them here,"

Padraic said. "I told you we're starting work on a barn. We'll need that to store feed for them and also as a place where they can shelter."

"Why'd you buy them from Bothwell?" I asked, trying not to show my disdain for him as I said his name.

Seamus gave me an odd look. "Who better? He knows me and he gave us a good price."

"You better check their hooves," I said, remembering that my father had always told me that one should do that. "If they're in good shape, the cow is probably in good shape too."

"I'm sure Bothwell will do us right," Seamus said.

I couldn't stop myself from saying, "I wouldn't be too sure about that."

Seamus gave me a look. "Hey, I worked for the fella, I should know. You got a thing against Bothwell?"

"I didn't say that."

"Well, you better get over it as we're having dinner with him tomorrow night, and I expect you to be your lovely self. He was always decent to me and he appears happy to help us get a start on our ranch." I just shook my head. "Brigid, we need his help," Seamus walked up close to me and lifted my head by the chin. "What we're going to try to do here is almost more work than we can accomplish. I know a lot from working with him, but I still have a lot more to learn. He can help us with all that."

Paddy stood up and handed me a beer. I took a swig and was glad for the rush of coolness down my throat. I knew I couldn't tell them what I had discovered about Ella's murder now. They wouldn't want to hear it and it would spoil their pleasure, which I did not want to do. And also, I was somewhat worried that they might try to stop me from confronting Bothwell with the evidence of how he was responsible for Ella's death and quite probably Bart's as well.

Seamus stood and held up his beer. "To our new livestock and to the man who sold them to us."

"I'll certainly drink to the cows," I added as we all clinked our bottles together.

After wiping his sleeve across his mouth, Seamus looked at me, all serious, and said, "Brigid, I'm telling you as your big brother, you need to behave when we dine at this fancy club."

Who knew what the definition of *behaving* was? All I knew was I pretty sure I knew how to handle Mr. Bothwell and was determined that the news of my find would come out in a way that he couldn't deny it.

37

We put up enough fence that we had all the new cattle out in the field late the next day. I was happy to see the beefy animals settling in, their long tails swishing through the grass, stirring up grasshoppers and the like. They would need more room, but this would keep them secure for now. I did suggest some names for the six of them—Daisy, Clover, Rose, Petunia, Shamrock, and Pansy—but Seamus and Padraic said no go.

"You can name the old gummer cow, but the rest of them won't need a name. They'll just be a number and produce some more stock for us."

I patted the old gummer on her forehead, which had a white mark like a half-moon in its center. "*Ghealach*," I said, the Irish word for moon.

"Such a romantic," Padraic said, patting me on the shoulder.

"She's a right *ijit*, if you ask me," Seamus joined in.

"Which we don't." I tried to kick my brother but he jumped out of the way.

Padraic held me back. "Watch out with him, Brigid. He's gotten mighty crusty on the trail."

❀   ❀   ❀

It was the big night of the dinner at the Cheyenne Club, and I had laid out all of our clothes, ready to go. I wound my hair up into a large topknot and let tendrils curl down in front of each ear. I so often wore it in a braid down my back that it felt odd for it to sit up high on my head, but I knew it was the style women were now wearing. As the final touch I placed my new small velvet hat with one dark plume on top of my hair and pinned it in carefully so it wouldn't move.

After spending quite a bit of time sewing a dark brown satin jacket, I had finished it just in time for this event. I carefully put it on and tried to see myself in the small looking glass I had leaned against a box on the table. I liked the feel of the new material on my arms, and the sleeves were slightly puffed, as was the latest fashion. The jacket went well with my dark black skirt that had a very slight bustle built into it. While I knew that my outfit might not be up to the standard of the glamorous outfits most women would be wearing at the club, I had been inspired by a pattern I had seen in an issue of *Godey's Lady's Book*. I dressed it up with a brooch at the neck and the lovely paisley shawl that I had been given by a suitor in Deadwood, one I no longer wanted to think about. I pulled on long leather gloves. I was ready to go. I made a face at myself in the mirror. It was the best I could do. I was both very excited to be going to the club and nervous. Into the side-seam pocket of my dress I tucked the piece of wool tweed I had found by the cottonwood tree. I daren't think about what I was going to do with it this night.

Thank goodness that Padraic had just bought a small carriage to drive us into town, for I certainly couldn't have ridden a horse in my outfit.

Padraic was wearing a dark suitcoat with a clean white shirt and looked quite smart. He had it buttoned so you couldn't see his vest. I hoped he might open it so that my handiwork would show. To top him, Seamus had on a light suitcoat over a white shirt and looked very grown up. I saw that my brother had become a handsome man and was glad of it. I would be proud to be on the arms of these two gentlemen at the club.

✻   ✻   ✻

A young boy rushed toward our carriage to attend it as Padraic brought the horse to a stop by one of the many hitching posts in front of the Cheyenne Club. Again I was awed by the look of this building, taking up a whole block in the downtown of Cheyenne. I couldn't believe I was actually going to have dinner there.

I had heard it also had tennis courts out back where only members were allowed to play. This was a new game that was coming into style, but

I had never had a chance to see it played. Maybe if I peeked through a window to the back I would see some balls being hit over a net.

Padraic helped me step down from the carriage and up the wide front steps. Some gentlemen were sitting in the chairs on the veranda, smoking big cigars and wearing their hats pushed back on their heads. They tipped their hats as we walked by and entered the main hall. I knew I was gawking, but I couldn't help standing still and just staring around at the stone work. I looked up and saw that the ceiling went up the full two stories and that it was decorated with stained glass so that light shone through it. It was all like a palace to me.

❊ ❊ ❊

"It's been called 'the pearl of the prairies.' We're very proud of it. As fine as anything you might see back in the states," Bothwell boasted as he led us to the dining room. "I'm one of the founding members. Only two hundred men are allowed to be members. They include graduates from Harvard, Princeton, and Yale. Even a few from Oxford. Quite exclusive."

On the way he stopped to show us the library with its well-stuffed dark leather chairs. The room was carpeted in an oriental rug and deep maroon curtains hung in the windows. I would have loved to enter the room, peruse the shelves of books, and sit in one of the chairs, perhaps reading the latest magazine that had come from the states out East. But on we went. Mr. Bothwell continued telling us of its grandeur, pointing out various rooms as we passed. "We have a billiards room, a wine vault, and even an elevator. Only members and their guests can make use of all these advantages."

Finally we came to the dining room, which was less grand than I expected and much more comfortable than I had thought it would be. The floors were dark hardwood covered with large Turkish carpets and the fireplace was tiled in rich colors with a perfect blaze showing off its interior. We were seated at a table set for five, and then introduced to Mr. Bothwell's wife, Clara. I looked across at this handsome woman with her dark hair streaked with gray and a touch of rouge on her cheeks. She looked very proud, as I supposed she must be, for how well her husband had done with his cattle business. The fineness of her clothing made me glad I had taken the time to sew myself my new jacket.

Menus were sitting by the side of each plate setting. I was impressed with the beauty of the script in which it was written and had a hard time deciding what I should choose to eat from all the choices. So many forms of meat—pork chops, roast quail, trout. Even something called Mock Turtle Soup, which I did not think I would try. Seamus pointed out one offering to me, Raw Oysters.

"I haven't had an oyster since I left Ireland," Seamus burst out.

Mr. Bothwell, who was sitting to his right, slapped him on the back and laughed. "Order them, by all means. They're shipped in from San Francisco. I thought we'd start with some champagne."

Champagne—even the sound of it brought a yearning to my mouth. I had had it only once before in Deadwood and I had found it, by far, the beverage of the gods. I couldn't help exclaiming, "How wonderful."

Mrs. Bothwell smiled at me and said, "I feel the same way."

As we were in beef country, I finally decided to order the roast beef, which came with Yorkshire pudding, whatever that was. After all, I should support Seamus and Padraic's endeavor—meat on the hoof.

After we gave our orders, the champagne arrived. I couldn't help remembering an earlier fancy dinner in Deadwood, when I was served champagne and then almost deflowered by my companion. I wondered where he was now and how he fared. I wished him little ill but never wanted to see him again.

"A toast," Mr. Bothwell lifted his glass. "To the future cattle barons of this fair land and to the sister they hold so dear."

How could I not drink to that?

There was pleasant chatter until the dinners started to be served. I felt in my pocket for the piece of wool. Then I forced myself to look across at Mrs. Bothwell, happily chatting away with Seamus. I wondered if she knew what her husband had done and if she condoned it. I hoped not, for her sake.

❋   ❋   ❋

What would I be ruining if I confronted Bothwell? Couldn't I just let it all be? Nothing I could do would change what had happened or bring Ella back. It would surely hurt Seamus to know this truth about his boss and certainly damage any chance he and Padraic had for getting help from Bothwell.

All the certainty and anger I had had when I saw the truth of Ella's murder was like to melt away. Here I was in this lovely room with the two men I loved most in the world. We were all of us ready to take on a new life that could lead to such good things: a home, a ranch, a marriage for me.

What if this troublesome piece of tweed wool could just be forgotten? Could I put it out of my mind? Would I be able to live with such a decision?

38

The plates had been cleared away, and I saw that Mr. Bothwell was looking around as if he were getting ready to leave us and seek out some of his fellow members to converse with. As I watched him, he turned and smiled at me as if we knew a secret together. I did not return his smile, for it was one of condescension and I could not stand it. He thought he could get away with what he had done, and in that moment I knew I could not stand to live without telling what I knew to be the truth.

Mr. Bothwell would be smiling no more. I knew it was time. I could put it off no longer.

I looked at his wife. She was patting her lips with her napkin and seemed quite content, like a cat who had finished a bowl of milk. She smiled over at me, and it was a true smile that said she was glad we were all there together. I hated to think what she would look like when I revealed what I knew. I turned away from her.

Mr. Bothwell stood and said that he must go excuse himself to talk to a few of the other members.

"Give me a moment," I asked. "I have something to say." And now there was no turning back.

He looked at me, first with wonder, then annoyance. "Surely, it can wait."

"No, I don't think so."

He sat down and I stood. I gripped the edge of the table and took a deep breath and let it out slowly. "I'm afraid I need to ask you about something, Mr. Bothwell. Something that I found yesterday."

"Why, my dear girl, ask away," he said leaning back and smiling at me like he was humoring me.

I pulled out the piece of wool tweed, held it up for all to see, then showed it to the Bothwells. "I found this yesterday."

Mr. Bothwell looked worried, but Mrs. Bothwell studied it for a moment, then smiled. "Oh, Brigid, that is grand. Why, wherever did you find that? It's off of Albert's new suitcoat. I noticed he had torn a pocket off when I was getting his clothes ready for tonight. Otherwise he would have worn that very coat. Thank you for finding it." She reached out her hand to take the fabric from me, but I pulled it back.

"I'm sorry but I'm not done." I couldn't let her have it. After all, it was evidence of a deadly crime.

Mr. Bothwell blanched and looked around for help. "I really don't think this is necessary. Is this what you wanted me to stay for?"

"Albert, not to worry. I'm sure that I can put the pocket back on your suitcoat." Again, Mrs. Bothwell reached over to take the piece, but I kept hold of it. "Please let me have it, my dear."

"I think you need to know first where I found it," I said, then asked her, "You know about the young woman who was hanged, yes?"

She stared at me for a moment, not understanding why I had brought up such a topic. "I didn't know her, but I have heard what happened, of course. A horrible thing," she said, her eyes growing larger. "But surely not something to be discussed at this fine dinner."

I continued, "Well, I disagree. You see, I found this scrap of wool by a tree out near her homestead. I found it right by to where I found her hanging. In fact, I found it under the tree she was hung from." Bothwell leaped up as if to grab the wool from my hands, but Padraic intercepted him and pushed him back down in his chair.

"What are you saying, Brigid?" Padraic asked. "You need to explain yourself immediately."

"I'm afraid you'll have to ask Mr. Bothwell how his suitcoat came to be torn at the scene of Ella's murder." I could hear anger in my voice. I knew it sounded out of place in this fine establishment, but when I thought of what he had done to Ella, I couldn't help myself. "Ask him how the pocket got torn from his coat."

"What do you have to say, Mr. Bothwell?" Padraic turned to him.

I watched Bothwell as his face suffused with rage. He tried to brush past Padraic while saying in a commanding voice, "Now listen, young lady, you can't go around suggesting such things. Why, do you know who I am?"

"I'm afraid I might, Mr. Bothwell. You are one of the big sugars and also the man who committed a murder, as far as I can tell. How else can you explain this pocket off your suitcoat being where I found it?"

Bothwell grew angrier and protested, "How dare you even suggest that I had anything to do with that incident. That's a very common fabric. Surely you can't think it came from me."

His wife looked at him, lifted her head up high, and said to me, "My husband is quite right. This all must be an awful coincidence. Someone else must have that same wool fabric."

"Yes, someone else does," I told her. "Me."

I turned to Padraic and asked him to open his coat and show them his vest.

There was a stunned silence until I continued. "I bought what remained of this particular tweed and made it into a vest. At that time, the merchant told me that your husband had been the first and only other buyer. So I'm afraid no one else has any of this specific fabric. This scrap must be from your husband's coat."

"Albert, what do you have to say?" His wife pulled away from him and asked, "Can you explain how this came to be?"

Mr. Bothwell pushed back his chair and stood as if to leave the table. He looked around the room but stayed where he was. "Explain? I have nothing to explain. This is sheer nonsense."

No one said anything. Seamus was looking down at his plate and Padraic grabbed my hand. "What are you doing?" he whispered to me.

Bothwell said loudly, "Why would I do such a thing? I have no reason to wish that woman ill."

"Yes, at first I thought the same," I answered him. "But then I heard that you had tried to buy her land." I waited, hoping to get a response from him.

He grabbed on to my statement and explained, "Yes, that's true. I made her an offer but she wouldn't hear of it, even when I offered much more than it was worth. She was a very stubborn woman."

"When a woman stands her ground, she is considered stubborn and worse. So, for that, you killed her?" I repeated. "To get her land?"

It was as if finally my words had hit him. He stammered as if he could not find words to explain, but finally he exploded. "You don't understand! It wasn't just that. She was also taking my calves right off the range. Ask the other ranchers," he insisted. "She had to be stopped."

"So you killed her?"

"In this here country stealing cattle is a hanging offense. I had every right to do what I did."

I had him. He had admitted it. But it gave me no pleasure.

There was dead silence at the table.

Seamus pushed his chair back from the table, and Padraic looked down at the floor. Mrs. Bothwell didn't seem to know where to look, and I watched her face turn pale from what she was hearing. "This can't be true," she said, just above a whisper. "My dear Albert, tell me this is all a lie."

Bothwell said nothing but sank into his chair.

"But you had no proof that she was making off with any of your cattle," I said. "How could you know that?"

"My men found an unmarked calf in her corral. Isn't that right, Jimmy?" Bothwell asked and looked at my brother.

"Jimmy," I whispered. He was asking for help from my brother. I had almost forgotten that he had this new nickname.

"Yes, Jimmy. If you want to know what happened out at the Bates homestead, all you have to do is ask your own brother," Bothwell said. "He was there. He was one of the gang. If I'm guilty, he is too."

I felt ill, broken. How could my brother be involved in such a horrible crime? He would never do such a thing. I couldn't take it in. "But he was not back yet. He was still out on the range. You weren't there, were you, Seamus?" I turned to him, hoping that he would tell me he had had nothing to do with Ella's death.

He hung his head and wouldn't look at me.

All the table was quiet.

I looked over at Padraic, and he turned away from me too. What did this mean? Why was he avoiding me? I had to ask. "What, Padraic? You knew of this? You knew what had happened to Ella?"

"Aye," he said in a low voice. "I did. Seamus told me about it himself when he arrived home. Before you got there."

I wanted to take my plate and throw it against the wall. I wanted to take my knife and stab Bothwell through the heart. I wanted to stand on the table and scream. But I did none of that.

Mrs. Bothwell, looking quite ill, suddenly said, "Is this true? Albert, you had this woman hanged by your men?" He looked away but didn't deny it.

Then louder, Mrs. Bothwell declared, no longer asking it as a question, "You had this poor woman lynched."

At that word, my heart stood still. *Lynched.* I could picture Ella struggling against this mob of men. *Lynched,* such a horrible, ugly word. I couldn't stand it. I got up quietly. "I can no longer be here." I pushed in my chair and started across the room.

Padraic ran after me and grabbed my arm. "Brigid, please listen. Seamus was only doing as he was ordered to by Bothwell. He feels mighty bad about what happened, that he does."

I looked at him, and even though we were standing in the middle of the fanciest restaurant in Cheyenne, I didn't care who heard what I had to say. "You knew, Paddy. While I was going around trying to find out how this had happened, you knew and you didn't tell me. You knew that Bothwell had Ella hanged and that my brother was a party to it—a lynching. How could you?"

He shook his head, not daring to look at me when he confessed. "At first I didn't know. Then, after he told me, I hoped it would never come out. I hoped you would never find out and it would all just go away."

"Padraic, how could you do that? Did you really think I'd never find out? You saw how hard I was trying to find out what had happened to Ella. How can I ever trust you again?" I shook off his arm and pushed him away.

The hurt I saw in his eyes couldn't stop me. Anger was welling up in me like a stoked-up fire and I felt ready to burst. "Don't come near me." And then, to hurt him, I told the biggest lie. "I never want to see you again."

Padraic fell back as if I had slapped him. The shock on his face spoke words. But I knew what I had to do and I was going to do it immediately, before I could change my mind. The sheriff's office was not far from the Cheyenne Club, and I set out to walk there before anyone could stop me.

39

There was no coming back from where I had gone, from what I had said, from what I had learned.

I walked down the street to the sheriff's office and told him the story—how one of the big sugars had decided to take the law into his own hands, even though Ella had done little wrong and ordered a group of his cowboys to string her up from a cottonwood tree in the plains.

I told him that there were witnesses to what Bothwell had done.

I told him that my brother could provide him with the rest of the names of the lynching party.

I gave him the piece of wool tweed and wished never to see it again.

"And you say that your brother will corroborate all this that you're telling me, that he worked for Bothwell."

"That's right. If you can go easy on him. He was under orders to help Bothwell in this killing."

"A terrible thing."

"Yes, it was."

He thanked me for my help and told me he would take care of it. "This is nothing for a young lady like you to be involved in."

I nodded and said he was right.

* * *

I couldn't go back to the soddy. There was no way I could face my brother or Padraic now. I also couldn't go back to stay at Dyer's Hotel. For one thing, I didn't want to chance running into Molly. As much as I wished her well, I did not want to see her crowing over what had happened with Padraic. And also, I didn't want to remember staying there with Padraic.

So I made the decision to take a room at the Intercontinental Hotel, the most expensive place in town. But why not? I had the money and I didn't think Padraic would think to look for me there.

The next day I would pull out money from the bank, pay my bill, and tell them where to send the rest. I would go back to the soddy and get my belongings and say my farewells.

❋ ❋ ❋

When I was alone in my grand hotel room, I threw myself down on the bed and cried until there was nothing left in me.

I had so wanted to be with Seamus again. We had followed him to Cheyenne and waited for him. Then my brother had rejoined us only to have me turn him in for a crime he had been told to commit. How had such a thing come to be? I dared not dwell on it.

And Padraic—I wasn't sure I could even look him in the eye again.

How I wished that I could turn back time, and the three of us could be sitting around a fire outside on the range, drinking beer and laughing and singing songs. Like we had been doing only a couple of days ago. Lying on the bed, wiping at my face, I even wished that I had never found that cursed piece of tweed. Or that I had thrown it into the fire. Or that I hadn't bought the same fabric myself and didn't know the significance of it. How I wished that it hadn't turned out the way it had.

But as my mam used to say, "Wish in one hand and spit in the other and see which one gets filled first." I missed her and my da and all my family. What would my father think of what I had done?

But it was done. And I needed to go on.

40

Two days later I quit Cheyenne.

I bought a ticket for Salt Lake City, which was the next big town to the west on the Union Pacific line. I wanted to leave as soon as possible, to get out of this town and away. I wondered what this city by an inland sea would be like. Mostly I wondered what the Mormons would be like. I had heard that the men could take more than one wife—*polygamy,* they called it. Sounded like a bad idea to me, then I wondered if it worked the other way around—if a wife could have more than one husband, not that I'd want more than one or maybe not even any.

When I boarded the train, the conductor said we would be to Salt Lake City in a little more than eight hours, which seemed amazing to me. I sat back in the comfort of my seat and watched the countryside move by. This mode of travel was so much superior to a stagecoach.

I looked down at my ring finger. There was a light-white band of skin where the Claddagh ring had been. To remove the ring I had had to soap my finger well and then slowly twist it off. The ring had not come away easily, but I must need to return it to Padraic.

My decision to leave had taken me a day or two to make. I had thought long and hard about what my life would be like if I stayed. But I finally understood that I had not come to America to be a rancher's wife, that I did not like the plains, that I hated living in a soddy. And I wasn't sure I could ever face my brother or Padraic again, certainly not live with them.

I started to dream about what I did want my life to look like . . . living in a city with bookstores and restaurants and maybe even close to water, a lake or the ocean even. No more dust, no more unceasing wind. To be my own person, to have a business that supported me. Surely this was not too much to ask.

The Great Salt Lake was the largest body of water between Cheyenne and the coast. I looked forward to seeing water again after living on the dusty plains.

I closed my eyes for a while on the train, the rocking on the rails sending me into sleep. I hadn't slept much in the past few days, and I felt totally spent.

*　＊　*

Before I left Cheyenne, I'd heard the news that the sheriff had arrested Albert Bothwell and my brother, too. I didn't care what happened to Bothwell, but I hoped in my heart that my brother wasn't given too hard a sentence. Even though he had been a party to the lynching, I needed to believe that he hadn't wanted to do it. That he had been only following orders. That he had believed Bothwell when he had told him that he had the right to hang Ella for cattle rustling.

*　＊　*

Padraic had been standing by the door to the soddy when the livery stable carriage brought me to the homestead. He opened the door of the carriage for me and helped me down without saying a word.

He stared at me. "Have you come back?" he finally asked.

"No, I haven't," I told him, tears filling my eyes.

"You staying in town?" he asked. Then his voice broke, and he said, "Oh, Brigid, won't you come back here with us? We can talk it out."

"No, I'm moving on."

He looked up at the sky. "I was afraid of that."

"I can't stay here. It's no good." I tried to think of words that would explain, but I couldn't find them.

"We could try—" He stopped himself from saying more.

I took the Claddagh ring from my pocket and gave it back to him. "I'm sorry, Padraic."

"Yes, as am I."

"I just can't."

"If that's the way it is." He shrugged his shoulders and shook his head.
"'Tis."

"Would it do any good for me to say how sorry I am?" he asked.

"It would make me feel better."

"You know I would never do anything to hurt you. I felt I owed an allegiance to Seamus when he told me what he had done. But I see now that in so doing, in keeping his secret, I wasn't being true to you. I wish I had done it all differently. I hope you know how sorry I am."

"I do," I whispered. I bent my head down so he wouldn't see my tears. "Thank you."

We went in the house together. I pulled my trunk out from under the table and hurriedly packed it with my few clothes. Padraic stood watching me but didn't utter a word. I too had nothing more to say, although words seemed to swirl around inside me, trying to find a way out.

When I stood up from putting the last of my belongings into the trunk, Padraic grabbed me around the waist and lifted me up and kissed me so hard I could not breathe, nor did I want to. It was all there, all we had felt for each other, all we were giving up.

❆ ❆ ❆

The carriage driver met us at the door and between Padraic and him they managed to carry my trunk to the wagon and put it in the back. The driver climbed up on his seat. Padraic and I stood together at the side of the carriage.

I reached up and stroked his cheek. I wanted to know his face forever. I studied his dark eyes, his sweet lips, his thick hair. I had come to know him so well, and I told him, "I've loved you so."

"I have loved you too. And I don't think I'll stop."

"Please give Seamus my love."

"I will."

I felt as if I were going to break, but I pulled myself together and said, "He's to have Grian. I've left a note for him. I know he will love her as much as I do. In the meantime, I know you will take good care of her. You know her almost as well as I do. Ride her gently."

"You'll write, won't you?" Padraic asked. "You'll tell us where you are and how you're faring."

"I will. I'll let you know where I land."

"I'll send you the news of the trial." He added, hopefully, "But, who knows, maybe there won't be one."

"Whatever happens I will hope for the best for my brother."

"I can't run this place without him."

I nodded.

"Pray for us, Brigid. But especially for me."

Then I looked up at him and told him truly, "With every breath."

Padraic grabbed my hands and held them tight. "Don't say goodbye to me, Brigid. Please don't."

I squeezed his hands. "No, I can't."

He let my hands fall, and I turned and climbed into the carriage by myself.

No last look at the home I was leaving, no last look at the man I had loved so deeply.

Author's Note

In 1889, twenty-eight-year-old Ellen Watson and her husband, James Averell, were corralled by a group of six men, taken to a large cottonwood tree by the banks of the Sweetwater, and lynched. This vigilante execution took place just miles outside the booming cattle town of Cheyenne, Wyoming. I learned of this lynching when I started my research for this second book of mine featuring Brigid Reardon. One of the many reasons I was writing a series of historical mysteries was that I had discovered I loved doing research, and while I wouldn't necessarily change a story to fit the historical truth, I was surprised to discover how often that truth already fit what I had planned to write.

What does the term *lynching* actually mean? It came into common parlance when a colonel during the American Revolution led illegal trials in Virginia to "combat outlawry" and he ordered people flogged for various crimes. His name was Charles Lynch, and such illegal justice became known as "Lynch Law" and took on more lethal forms of punishment.

Then, in 1940, a meeting of antilynching organizations came together to create a more concise definition of the term. They determined that *lynching* was "a killing outside the bounds of the law committed by a group, usually of three or more individuals, acting 'under the pretext of service to justice, race, or tradition.'"

In the west of the United States, lynching occurred for different reasons and to different people from those in the southern states, where most lynchings were the end result of racial violence. Livestock rustling was often the reason for such an action in the west. In his book on lynchings, W. Fitzhugh Brundage reports that 447 whites and 38 Blacks were lynched in the far American West between 1880 and 1930. And the lynching of a woman was not as unusual as we might think: Kerry Segrave, in his book on the lynching of women, found that between 1851 and 1946, ninety Black women, nineteen white women, and six women of unknown racial background were lynched.

After reading the true story of Ellen Watson's lynching, I knew I wanted to write about it in the second tale of Brigid's travels in America. Watson, also known as Cattle Kate, was the only woman known to have been lynched in Wyoming. The leader of the mob who killed her was Albert Bothwell, one of the big sugars of Cheyenne. He claimed that "Ella" and James had stolen yearling calves off the range before they had been branded and slipped them into their own herd. This was not an unusual way to procure more cattle in those days and was even jokingly called getting them by the "longest rope."

However, it seems clear that the real reason behind the lynching was that Bothwell wanted to add their land to his ranch. The cattle barons of this time were so powerful that while Bothwell and his crew were tried for the lynching, they were not convicted of it. An article in the *Cheyenne Daily Leader* explained: "The attorneys for the territory, Messrs. Craig and Howard seemed to have done all in their power to secure the necessary evidence and the facts were fully presented to the jury as far as they were obtainable, but without avail."

I used some of the facts about this historical lynching in my book and kept the names of Ella and Bothwell, but I did not stick exactly to their story. This is a work of fiction playing off a real-life happening—which, when you think about it, is what many novels do.

❋   ❋   ❋

Many thanks to all who supported me in this journey: Pete Hautman, the first and most severe critic of all my writing and the love of my life; Erik Anderson, a true gentleman and a most thoughtful editor; Nancy St. Clair, best friend since seventh grade and a careful reader; my sister Dodie Logue, who knows her horses and is a great traveling companion; and Ruth LaFortune, my wonderful pharmacist sister who helps me understand which poison might be most effective, among other things.

Many thanks to the University of Minnesota Press, both for publishing books that are off the beaten track and for doing such a beautiful job of it.

References

Brundage, W. Fitzhugh. *Lynching in the New South: Georgia and Virginia, 1880–1930*. Urbana: University of Illinois Press, 1993.

Moses, Christopher Waldrep. *Lynching in America: A History in Documents*. New York: New York University Press, 2006.

O'Neal, Bill. *Cheyenne: A Biography of the "Magic City" of the Old West, 1867–1903*. Austin, Tex.: Eakin Press, 2006.

Segrave, Kerry. *Lynchings of Women in the United States: The Recorded Cases, 1851–1946*. Jefferson, N.C.: McFarland, 2010.

Mary Logue has published more than thirty books, including mystery novels, poetry, nonfiction, and books for children. She has received a Minnesota Book Award, a Wisconsin Outstanding Achievement Award, and an Edgar nomination. Her previous Brigid Reardon mystery, *The Streel,* was a WILLA literary award finalist for historical fiction; her poetry book *Meticulous Attachment* received a Midwest Booksellers honor award; and her picture book *Sleep Like a Tiger* won a Charlotte Zolotow honor, a Caldecott honor, and Best Picture Book award in Japan. She has taught in writing programs at the University of Minnesota and Hamline University and has written for the *New York Times,* the *Star Tribune,* and the *Village Voice.* She lives in Golden Valley, Minnesota, and Stockholm, Wisconsin.